"TRUST ME," C.J. SAID.

Jason stared at her a long moment, wondering if he dared take that leap of faith. Her eyes pleaded with him for something he didn't know if he could give. But then his arms settled around her. "I do. God help me, I know it's a mistake, but I do trust you."

She asked softly, "Why is it a mistake?"

His hands snuggled her even closer before he tipped her chin up to meet his gaze. "Because you don't yet trust me enough to tell me the truth."

The sudden wariness in her eyes confirmed his assertion. She was holding something back. What, he didn't know. But at this moment he wasn't even sure he cared. He took a deep breath and said, "Just one thing. Do you want me?"

C.J. smiled. This question was the easiest in the world to answer.

"Yes," she said, slipping her arms around his neck. "I want you. I want you most of all. More than anything. More than my next breath. More than—"

His mouth stopped the flow of words in a kiss. . . .

WHAT ARE *LOVESWEPT* ROMANCES?

They are stories of true romance and touching emotion. We believe those two very important ingredients are constants in our highly sensual and very believable stories in the LOVE-SWEPT line. Our goal is to give you, the reader, stories of consistently high quality that may sometimes make you laugh, sometimes make you cry, but are always fresh and creative and contain many delightful surprises within their pages.

Most romance fans read an enormous number of books. Those they truly love, they keep. Others may be traded with friends and soon forgotten. We hope that each LOVESWEPT romance will be a treasure—a "keeper." We will always try to publish

LOVE STORIES YOU'LL NEVER FORGET
BY AUTHORS YOU'LL ALWAYS REMEMBER

The Editors

Loveswept ®871

NEVER SAY
GOOD-BYE

MAUREEN
CAUDILL

BANTAM BOOKS
NEW YORK · TORONTO · LONDON · SYDNEY · AUCKLAND

NEVER SAY GOOD-BYE
A Bantam Book / January 1998

ISBN 0-553-44556-1

Published simultaneously in the United States and Canada

Bantam Books are published by Bantam Books, a division of Bantam Dou-
bleday Dell Publishing Group, Inc. Its trademark, consisting of the words
"Bantam Books" and the portrayal of a rooster, is Registered in U.S. Patent
and Trademark Office and in other countries. Marca Registrada. Bantam
Books, 1540 Broadway, New York, New York 10036.

PRINTED IN THE UNITED STATES OF AMERICA
OPM   10 9 8 7 6 5 4 3 2 1

To Judy Veisel, friend and critique partner. May your guardian angel protect you, even when, as now, life simply isn't fair.

Dear Reader,

I have a confession to make. Like the heroine of this book, I'd never watched the classic movie *It's a Wonderful Life* all the way through. Oh, sure, bits and pieces here and there, the clips that get shown with every Jimmy Stewart retrospective or each commercial advertising the next televised viewing. But sit down and watch the whole movie? Not me. Too smarmy. Too . . . *too.*

But then, while planning this book, I watched it beginning to end. And you know what? It's a marvelous film! Great characters, great conflict, a charming small-town setting; the story has everything.

So that set my creative juices flowing. What if it weren't the hero who was so determined to "shake the dust of this crummy little town" from his feet? What if . . .

And thus another story is born.

Enjoy!

Maureen Caudill

ONE

Why did disasters invariably strike on Friday afternoons? Jason Cooper speared his fingers through his hair and stared at the letter crumpled in his other hand. This wasn't a normal business calamity, like a major distribution snafu or an important customer canceling their account. He could have coped with either of those. But this—this called for nothing less than flat-out retreat.

Unless he could figure a way to get out of the situation . . .

"What's up, Jase?" Rome Novak, Jason's brother-in-law and boss at the San Diego corporate headquarters of Golden Auto Parts, sauntered into Jason's office.

Jason ignored the slight scent of grape Popsicle du Jour that clung to the otherwise impeccably dressed Rome. He had already noticed that being daddy to toddler triplets sometimes generated compromises in Rome's personal grooming. "Have you seen this?" He thrust the letter at Rome.

After scanning the page, Rome tossed it onto the smallest pile on Jason's cluttered desk. "Sure. The editor at *California Business* magazine called me about it last week. Didn't I mention it to you? I told her to arrange things with your secretary—and I guess she has." An innocent smile lit up Rome's face.

"You *knew* about this? And didn't warn me?" Jason was beginning to suspect a plot. Cora Greene, his intimidating secretary, hadn't breathed a word about it, which meant that Rome must have conned her into keeping the arrangements secret. It wasn't the first time she'd conspired with Rome "for Jason's own good." One of these days he was going to have to fire her for lack of respect—or something. As soon as he got up the nerve.

In the meantime, at least he could protest to the true source of his woes. Rome. "I can't believe you committed me to this. Now I've got to let this writer follow me around for a whole week!"

"Well, at least they're sending a female writer. When I was given the honor five or six years ago, my tagalong interviewer was a guy who was Medicare eligible. With the sniffles." Rome chuckled ruefully. "Besides, what's wrong with being dubbed the Sexiest Businessman in California? As I recall, it was a lot of fun."

"No way." Jason was positive about this. "Are you claiming you *enjoyed* the prying into your personal life that resulted from that stupid title? I know being labeled 'Sexiest Anything' sounds like any guy's fantasy. Ha! Nightmare is more like it from what I saw."

"Maybe it wasn't *all* fun and games," Rome conceded, "but it wasn't all that bad. Besides, business doubled almost overnight, which generated enough extra cash to take the franchise nationwide." He shrugged. "I figured it was worth whatever inconveniences—"

"Inconveniences? *Inconveniences?*" Jason whirled to stare out the window and shoved his hands into his pants pockets. "If it was so damn minor a problem, why did you call me in a panic at one A.M. because three so-called ladies had you cornered in that bar up in Mission Viejo?"

Behind him, Rome's feet shuffled uncharacteristically. "Uh, Jase? You never told Lyssa about that little situation—did you?"

Sending an exasperated glance at his sister's husband, Jason turned to lean against the edge of the window. He shook his head. "Married life is obviously destroying your memory. Have you forgotten that it was written up, complete with color photos, in the *Union-Tribune*? Made quite a splash when the four of you ended up in the fountain."

Rome winced at the all-too-accurate pun. "No wonder Lyssa was convinced I'd make a terrible husband."

"Well, she was wrong. I couldn't have picked a better brother-in-law myself. But that Sexiest Businessman title sure as hell didn't help your case any."

Rome's gaze pierced Jason. "Is that what concerns you? Are you worried that some girl you're dating will shy off if you go along with this?"

"No, of course not. I'm not seeing anyone seriously right now."

Rome smiled. "Then you've got nothing to worry about."

"Yes, I do," Jason insisted. "You know that *California Business* was bought out a few months ago. I'm sure I mentioned it to you when I saw the article in *Investor's Daily*."

Rome's feet shuffled again in an I-want-out-of-here dance. "And your point is?"

"The point is that Solomon Mooney is the man who bought it. The same Solomon Mooney who also owns such stellar rags as *Spy on You* and *Gossip*. Rumor is, he's going to give *California Business* the same treatment, turning it into a tabloid scandal sheet."

But Rome wasn't buying it. "Yeah, maybe. But those 'rags' you mentioned have two of the highest circulations in the country. If he does the same with *California Business*, you'll get lots of exposure."

"Exposure is exactly what I *don't* want!" Jason raked his hand through his hair so violently, he was absently surprised not to find a fistful of it tangled in his fingers.

Rome gave him a sly glance. "Look, Jase, when this writer"—he glanced at the letter on the desk—"C. J. Stone shows up this afternoon, just play along. Who knows? Maybe having your profile appear in *California Business* will double our profit margin again. After all, I did it—why can't you?" He tapped his chin speculatively. "But then, I am better-looking than you."

"Says who?"

"Lyssa," Rome said smugly. "Ten bucks says you're not a big enough draw to double the company's again."

Jason's competitive spirit reared its head. "If business did double, it would be a greater accomplishment than you pulled off. We're a whole lot bigger now than back then."

"You're only saying that because you don't think you can stand up to my record. How about this? Ten bucks says you can't generate even a fifty percent rise in sales."

"You're on!"

Rome grinned and left the office, whistling.

Jason groaned as the realization of what had just occurred sank in. Suckered again. Damn.

When would he learn that betting with Rome inevitably led to disaster?

Now he was stuck. He had to cooperate with *California Business*. Rome had committed him— and more important, Golden Auto Parts—to it. He glared at the letter again.

Sexiest Businessman in California. Hmmph. Okay, so it *was* a major ego stroke. But he sure as hell didn't want his life disrupted by having something like that blazoned in headlines.

He dropped into the chair behind his desk and stared moodily at the letter. Rome's promise to the magazine locked Jason into cooperating with C. J. Stone. But if it was too late to convince the writer to leave him alone for the next week, maybe he could do something else . . . like make a solid case that he *wasn't* the Sexiest Businessman after all. Then the magazine would simply have to find someone else to persecute.

Of course, he'd lose his bet with Rome—a bet he'd been tricked into—but it would be worth more than the ten bucks to keep his private life just the way he liked it. Private.

An unholy grin spread across his face as he rapidly considered his conclusion. That was it. All he had to do was change his image for a week. How hard could that be? Sexy was definitely out. And what was the opposite of sexy? Why, bland. Dull. B-o-r-i-n-g.

Applying all his management skills to the problem, Jason rapidly constructed his strategy to transform himself into the Most Boring Businessman in California.

C. J. Stone was late. After a quick trip to the men's room to adjust his appearance, Jason impatiently drummed his fingers. He glanced at his watch for the third time in three minutes, confirming that Ms. Stone definitely could use a lesson in punctuality.

Just as he reached for the phone to make sure the writer wasn't cooling her heels in the lobby, someone rapped on his office door. A moment later Cora opened it and poked her head inside.

"C. J. Stone from *California Business* magazine is downstairs waiting to—what did you do to yourself?"

He groaned. He'd forgotten that his secretary would see his new look too. And comment on it. "I just wanted to spiff up a bit for the interview. Is that all right with you?" He gave her his best intimidating glare.

Naturally, it bounced right off her. After all, she was a lot more experienced at intimidation than he was. Jason wasn't too sure how old the stylish and carefully made-up Cora was. He figured from the tiny wrinkles around her eyes that she was at least forty-five, and maybe as much as sixty. He only knew her ferocious efficiency sometimes made him shake in his boots.

And despite the informality with which Rome

ran Golden Auto Parts, she persistently refused to address him as anything less formal than "Mr. Jason"—a title that made him feel like a nine-year-old who'd just broken yet another window with a stray fly ball.

Which, he supposed, was precisely why she called him that.

"Don't you give me that I'm-the-boss look," she said. Leaving the office door open, she marched over to stand beside his chair, where she eyed him up and down, her hands perched on her hips. "You look terrible."

"Gee, thanks. I thought I cleaned up pretty well."

Cora's eyes rolled skyward. "Men. That writer's on her way up here and you look like a— a—"

"A what?" Interested, he waited for her to come up with a description of his Mr. Boring look.

"A hamster, that's what! You call this spiffing up for an interview? Well, I can fix things—it'll just take a minute."

Without waiting for permission, she spun his chair around to face her. With the ruthlessness of a mother doing a clean-ears check, she brusquely ran her hand over his carefully water-slicked, parted-in-the-middle hair until he felt the strands falling into their usual side part. His sputtered protests and attempts to evade her ministrations received no more attention than a car gives a windshield-splatted bug.

In another moment she snatched off the clip-on bow tie he'd borrowed from someone in accounting and tossed it into a desk drawer. She was muttering how some men had no idea how to dress to impress while she freed the first couple of buttons of his shirt, when a cough sounded at the door.

"Uh, excuse me. Are you Jason Cooper?"

Simultaneously Jason and Cora froze. He didn't have to look to know that C. J. Stone had just walked in and found him with his secretary standing intimately between his knees unbuttoning his shirt, and his hands hanging on to her wrists. No doubt he looked sufficiently disheveled for Ms. Stone to imagine all kinds of misbehavior. He could only hope that Cora's usual immaculate grooming and frosty manner belied the obvious conclusions.

Slowly, he turned his head to face the doorway. Sure enough, a clearly amused woman leaned against the doorjamb, her stylish brown bob gleaming gold and amber in a ray of sunlight. She looked the image of professionalism in slim-cut pleated fire-engine-red slacks, a silky cream blouse, and a matching red blazer—far more professional than Jason felt at the moment.

"Am I interrupting something . . . important?" she asked disingenuously.

He released Cora's hands and swiveled his

chair to face the intruder. Mistake number two. His left kneecap caught the red-faced Cora behind her right knee and tumbled the older woman into a wriggling heap in his lap.

"*Mr. Jason!* That is *quite* enough!" Cora's protests tangled with Jason's hands as he tried to lever her back into a standing position.

"Oh, hell." Helpless to find a smooth, professional, utterly *boring* way out of this fiasco, Jason abruptly stood, almost knocking the gasping Cora to the floor. He helped her regain her balance, then stepped around the desk, trying to look as if he didn't spend every Friday afternoon wrestling with his secretary.

"Hello, Ms. Stone," he said, holding out his hand and putting on his best winning smile, "I'm Jason Cooper."

"So I see." Her brisk handshake warmed his fingers. Intelligence shimmered in her gold-brown eyes and competency clung to her like perfume. Not a lady to bamboozle easily.

But wouldn't it be fun trying? His heart thumped hard, and he hastily withdrew his hand from hers.

"Mr. Jason, I'll leave you and Ms.—Ms.—"

Cora's interruption flooded him with unexpected relief, as it drew his attention back to his secretary. For the first time in Jason's memory, she was flustered enough to forget a visitor's name. Cora patted her skirt and jacket into pristine neatness while she strode toward the door.

"Stone. C. J. Stone." Damn, but the writer's husky voice reminded him of the hot apple cider he'd loved as a kid: warm, smooth, with just a hint of spice.

"Yes. Stone. That's right." Visibly pasting her composure back together, Cora paused just inside the office to give Jason a you-won't-be-forgiven-this-for-a-while glare. "I'll leave you and *Master* Jason now."

Jason winced. Please don't let C.J. ask about the title Cora just bestowed on him, he prayed silently. A firm click of the door punctuated Cora's escape as he silently indicated a chair and leaned against his desk. *Please don't let her ask.*

But C.J.'s eyebrow arched as she said, " 'Master' Jason? Sounds like your management style could use a little update." Her gaze took in his mussed hair and his shirt, which Jason now noticed had slipped another button or two, leaving his chest half-bare. "In more ways than one."

Resigned, Jason buttoned his shirt. "I suppose you'd like to hear an explanation?"

"Have you thought up a good one yet?" C.J. settled comfortably in the chair, crossing her legs and displaying an interested, though completely skeptical expression.

"Aw, hell. It's not like that. I was just—" *Trying to make myself look boring so you'd choose someone else as the Sexiest Businessman?* Yeah, right. She'd sooner believe he was a space alien. He tried again. "She didn't mean 'master' as in *master*. It's her way of chastising me. Like you might address a little kid . . . Master Billy? Master Jason? See what I—you're not buying any of this, are you?"

C.J. watched Jason squirm under her direct gaze. Sexy wasn't the only word that described Jason Cooper. Alluring. Enticing. Even downright irresistible. With a sigh, she dragged her professionalism back in place.

"Would you like to start again, Mr. Cooper?" she asked, unable to restrain a grin as she held out her hand. "Hello, I'm C. J. Stone from *California Business* magazine. We have an appointment at two o'clock."

Again, his fingers wrapped around hers. Again, as she had during their first handshake, she felt the heated thump-thud of her heart as she shook his hand briefly.

"Call me Jason. I'm, uh, sorry about the, uh . . ." He gestured vaguely as if encompassing the entire situation.

Her grin turned into a smile. "Think nothing of it. Did the magazine editors explain how I'll be working with you for the next week?"

Warm hazel eyes stared into hers for a long moment as if he hadn't heard her question. Then he visibly pulled himself together. "Yes. Sure. Look, let me make myself presentable again, and we'll start."

He straightened, keeping an obvious distance from her chair, and took a step toward the door, then swiveled suddenly, retreated behind his desk, and pulled something from a drawer. Almost before C.J. could take two breaths, Jason had walked out of the office with a determined stride.

Was it something I said? C.J. shook her head and waited, wondering what was going on with the undoubtedly sexy but obviously distracted man. Pulling out a pad, she began reviewing her notes for the interview. She'd barely begun when Jason reentered the office.

At least she thought it was Jason Cooper. The shirt looked familiar, even if it was now buttoned to his chin, but what happened to the sensually tousled brown hair? And where had that bow tie come from? Instead of male cover-model material, she faced a man who looked like Hugh Grant on one of his less assertive days.

And while some women sighed over Grant's hypersensitive indecisiveness, C.J. thought the man a wimp.

"Sorry about that, Ms. Stone. I just wanted to make myself a little more presentable." Even his voice had lost its husky warmth, its tone now one of bland inoffensiveness.

Had Jason just had a major personality transplant, like some modern-day Dr. Jekyll and Mr. Hyde? "Call me C.J.," she said slowly, still trying to figure out what was going on. "I'm sorry if my presence has disrupted your day."

"No problem. I'm, uh, very grateful that your magazine wants to, uh, name me as, uh, the, um, sexiest"—did his voice actually *crack* merely saying the word?—"businessman, but surely there are, er, lots of others who—not that I mind, of course, but, uh, don't you think that . . ."

C.J.'s mouth dropped open as she sat, completely astonished at the flood of useless words coming from Jason Cooper's mouth. What had happened to the dynamic man she'd interrupted practically in flagrante delicto with his secretary?

She cut through his ramblings. "You *are* Jason Cooper, aren't you? Executive vice-president of Golden Auto Parts?"

He nodded.

A grim smile touched her mouth. "You're it, then. California's sexiest businessman."

"Er, if you say so."

"More to the point, my editors say so. It's up to me to convince the rest of our readership that the editors are right."

"Tough job, huh?" he said, a gleam of humor lighting his eyes at her determined, not-very-optimistic tone.

She remembered her cardinal rule of interviewing just in time: Never insult the subject of your interview. "Why, not at all!" But then she blew it with her unthinking follow-up. "I thrive on challenges, Jason. I really do."

How on earth was she going to make this man sound like the sexiest thing since snug, button-fly jeans when his real personality was definitely more suited to baggy bibbed overalls?

By the time C.J. had completed the initial interview with Jason, she was convinced she'd somehow gotten lost inside a Kurt Vonnegut novel. Nothing made any sense. Her every question was met with an answer innocuous enough to pass a Senate confirmation hearing. She had an hour of taped material and pages of notes, none of which would be useful in the slightest. How could she produce an interesting, sexy profile of a man who apparently had the pizzazz of a bowl of tapioca?

What was she going to do?

Jason had invited her to observe him at work—he was in charge of the office, he'd said, since Rome Novak was taking his usual Friday afternoon off to spend time with his kids. But he'd done little more than shuffle a few papers on his desk and answer two phone calls, one of which was obviously a request to stop at the grocery store on the way home.

"Do you have a steady relationship with someone?" she'd asked after that call. She already knew Jason wasn't married. It was one of the prerequisites to being named sexiest businessman. A man with a live-in lover, she reasoned, must have some degree of sexuality—but whatever she'd thought she'd seen in Jason when she'd surprised him with his secretary had totally disappeared by the time he'd donned that awful bow tie.

"What? Oh, the call? Not exactly. My sister Lyssa wants me to drop some groceries off on my way home—I live only a block or two from her and Rome. I did tell you that Rome's my brother-in-law, didn't I? Well, he took their kids to the zoo this afternoon and won't be back in time. To go to the grocery store, I mean."

Poof! There went *that* hope. And would she ever be able to cut through the torrent of words he spewed with every question?

"What kind of woman attracts you, Jason?" Surely any man would perk up given free rein to answer a question like that!

He carefully shuffled one paper under another, then straightened the stack before answering. "I like nice women. Ladies. Someone I could introduce to my mother."

Oh, help. C.J. was almost ready to throw in the towel when she caught him peeking at her, assessing her reaction to his claim. Was he *testing* her somehow? If so, why?

Deliberately, she put on an approving smile. "So you're interested in getting married?"

"Of course! I'm definitely planning to marry someday."

Shocked by his immediate agreement—almost the only unequivocal answer he'd given all afternoon—she realized he'd been surprised by her question. But before she could frame a follow-up question, his telephone rang and she lost the moment.

Great. A man with a body to die for and a personality as boring as her high-school algebra textbook. Not to mention the fashion sense of a salamander, she mentally added, checking out the ugly brown-and-yellow bow tie one more time. How could she make this article come alive to the reader when watching him shuffle papers could be trumpeted as a surefire cure for insomnia?

It was important for her to do a knock-your-socks-off profile. This assignment was her swan song for *California Business* magazine, and she wanted it to be her best work. Her letter of resignation was burning a hole on the hard disk of her laptop computer. If her luck held—superstitiously, she crossed her fingers—she could deliver the letter at the same time she turned in the completed profile of Jason Cooper.

She only needed written confirmation from *International Living* with the final terms of their job offer, and she'd be flying off to assignments in glamorous resorts all over the world. After all, she'd stayed at *California Business* for almost eighteen months—a new record for her. Her feet already itched from the urge to sever ties and get on to new places and new people.

Of course, *International Living* wasn't exactly

the career move of her dreams. The magazine lavished its attention on the very rich, people whose lives were so single-mindedly devoted to conspicuous consumption that they served as marvelously bad examples for the rest of the world.

She'd once longed to do serious work, and had even toyed with taking a leave of absence from *California Business* to work on that book project that was gathering dust at the back of her desk. But then *IL* had expressed serious interest in her writing, and she figured she could always work on that book some other time—sometime after sipping champagne and nibbling caviar as a predinner snack grew tiresome. So, once that *IL* offer came in, she was off for the bright lights and luxurious homes of the rich-and-wannabe-famous.

Jason had swiveled his chair to stare out the window behind her while he spoke on the phone. Abruptly, he hung up and stood, jerking her attention back to him. "Excuse me, C.J. I have to leave you for a little while. Ask Cora for anything you want." Without waiting for a reply, he once again strode out of the office.

This time, however, C.J.'s instincts screamed at her to follow. Something was up, and she had a strong feeling that the steely-eyed Jason Cooper who'd just left was closer to the sexy man she'd caught canoodling with his secretary than the passionless automaton she'd been struggling to render interesting.

She was only three steps behind him as he dashed down the hall and took the stairs two at a time. By the time they left the building, she was almost running in her attempts to keep up.

"Ohmigod!" She skidded to a stop when she realized Jason was headed to the warehouse building next door.

Smoke and flames were pouring from the roof of the Golden Auto Parts warehouse—a fire that obviously would have been easily visible from Jason's office window.

But as she stared she realized that Jason was still barreling toward the inferno.

"You can't go in there!" She dashed forward and pulled his arm until he, too, was forced to stop. "It's too dangerous!"

He glared at her, all male determination. "I have to. We may still have some people trapped inside."

"But . . . wait till the fire department gets here." She caught the faint wail of sirens in the distance. "They're on the way and they know what they're doing. It's too dangerous!"

He shook off her restraining grip. "By that time it might be too late." Quickly he stripped off his shirt and wrapped it over his nose and mouth to serve as a mask. He gave her a nudge away from the building. "Go down by the end of the driveway and direct the fire engines when they get here. Go!"

Without watching to see if she obeyed, Jason dashed toward the burning building, pulled open the door, and ducked inside.

TWO

It was the dumbest—and the bravest—act C.J. had ever witnessed. She stared hard at the door Jason had gone into while visions of rusty-armored knights and tattered windmills danced in her mind. Somehow, she was convinced that as long as she didn't take her eyes from that door, he'd be safe.

The depth of her concern shocked her. She barely knew the man—and what she did know of him she found contradictory and confusing. She'd had a lifetime of experience maintaining her distance from others, and more than enough reason to make it a deep-rooted, permanent policy. So why was she blinking back tears? Why did her hands shake?

Why did she care?

With an angry swipe across her eyes, she tried to rub away her concern. She merely wanted to do a good job. That was it. Her worry wasn't *personal*, just the normal concern anyone would have for someone performing a valiant, if utterly reckless, deed.

Nonetheless she kept her gaze on that door.

Peripherally, she noticed that a crowd of people had gathered. Stopping the nearest person—Cora Greene, as it happened—C.J. said, "Jason wants someone to go down the drive and direct the fire trucks. Can you do that?"

"Of course. Where is he?"

C.J. hesitated, still keeping her attention on that door. Obviously Jason and this woman shared some kind of relationship—should she explain about his rash plunge into heroism? "The sirens are getting closer. Someone needs to be there to direct them. Go quickly!"

She felt more than saw Cora's nod and departure. *She had to keep watching that door.* Despite her concentration, her professional instincts sent her fingers fumbling in her oversized bag to pull out a small camera.

The fire engines wailed, then filled the air with their silence, and the crowd mushroomed again. Slicker-covered firemen hustled into action, smoothly preparing to fight the flames bursting through one corner of the building.

C.J. grabbed the first to come within reach and yelled, "There are people still in the building! Someone just went in that door to try to rescue them."

The firefighter nodded grimly, shouted orders at his fellow firefighters, and stepped up his activity.

On automatic pilot, C.J. snapped photos of the scene, without removing her attention from that stubbornly closed door.

What if he couldn't get out?

Two firemen approached the door warily, testing it for heat before cracking it open. C.J.'s breath stuck in her throat. Would they find Jason? Would he be safe?

Smoke billowed from the door, making the firemen pause. But through the smoke a soot-grimed, bare-chested figure emerged, carrying one person over his shoulder and leading a second. Jason!

She'd recognize that brawny chest anywhere. It was definitely Jason.

"Everyone's out now!" His voice, husky from smoke and fumes, reassured the firefighters as he guided his flock of rescuees to the waiting paramedics.

Her fears subsiding, she allowed herself to slip back into her professional role, using her camera to record each dazed expression on the faces of the survivors. Smoke twitched at her nose, an all-too-vivid reminder of the danger Jason had braved. With every snick-whirr of the shutter, her feet carried her closer to Jason as he gently placed his burden on a stretcher and guided the other person, a teenage boy, to a second stretcher.

By the time she stood next to him, she was sure her journalistic objectivity was fully in place again. Yet when he pulled his blackened shirt away from his nose and mouth and grinned at her in triumph, she suddenly wanted to slap him silly.

"What the *hell* did you think you were doing? Trying to get yourself killed?"

His grin faded and he studied her, those warm hazel eyes serious. "No," he said. "I was trying to keep other people from being killed. That's our warehouse and our people inside. It was my responsibility to get them out if I could."

She met him glare for glare before backing down. Mentally batting away the angry relief that bubbled within her, she forced herself to remember why she was there. The profile article. It had to be the best one she'd ever written. And with this act of idiotic heroism, her only problem was going to be making Jason Cooper appear less like an idiot and more like a hero.

"At least I'm not going to have much trouble making you sound good for the magazine," she muttered, turning away. "A genuine hero is about as sexy as it gets."

She focused hard on the burning building again. Even to her eyes, filling again with a surge of unaccountable tears, it was clear the firemen had already subdued the flames. It's just the soot, she assured herself as she surreptitiously wiped away a trickle of moisture.

What else could it be?

The adrenaline rush that had kept Jason going receded as C.J. turned away, leaving him swaying. *He'd forgotten about that article.* Damn. All he'd had to do was be bland and inoffensive for one lousy week and he'd blown it the first afternoon.

But that didn't mean he couldn't regroup and recover. Hell, a good manager could always turn a disaster into a success—and he was a very good manager.

Glancing around, he saw news trucks from the local TV stations pulling into a nearby parking lot and the hordes of reporters stampeding his way.

He tugged C.J. away from the paramedics' truck. "Let's get out of the way. I have to let Rome know what's happening and see about cleaning up this mess. And find another shirt." The last was added as he caught her surreptitious peek at his chest.

The slight flush along the side of her neck might have been from the fast pace he maintained, but he didn't think so. *Interesting.* He stifled a flare of masculine speculation and concentrated on the more immediate task of repairing the damage already done, both to the company and to his personal goal of convincing

C. J. Stone that he was really Mr. Dull-and-Worthy.

By the time Jason was finally ready to go home, it was long past his usual quitting time. The major problems of the fire had ben settled. Luckily, the most serious damage was limited to one corner of the warehouse. No one had been badly hurt, and although the two people he'd brought out of the building were rushed to the hospital, both had already been released with no significant injuries.

He'd even managed to grab a quick shower in the executive washroom and had changed into a pair of sweats and a comfortable knit shirt he kept in his office. Since his nerdy disguise was a total loss from soot, smoke, and several stray singe marks, he'd slam-dunked it into the trash.

All he really wanted now was to go home, pop open an icy brew, and maybe catch a good movie.

Unfortunately, no one had bothered to tell his tagalong writer that she should go home too. She could have given stick-to-his-side lessons to a tube of epoxy as she followed him relentlessly, silently absorbing every decision he made and snapping her endless photos. Her expression had changed from dubious to smug over the past several hours as his Mr. Bland persona went up in smoke.

He trudged to his car, mentally scrambling for a way to retrieve his control over the situation. He was only trying to keep his life simple and uncomplicated, and the last thing he wanted was to be turned into the latest of some gossip rag's fifteen-minute celebrities.

Then C. J. Stone appeared, and suddenly he was discovered compromising his secretary—Cora Greene, of all people!—and fire broke out, and he played the damned hero, and—it simply wasn't fair!

Ruefully, he pressed the button on his key chain to unlock his car and turned to stare at C.J., who had followed him out to the parking lot. Of course.

"I suppose you'll be heading for your hotel now, right?" Could he help it if his voice held a hopeful note?

"You don't have a, um, social engagement for this evening?" she asked.

Leaning his forearm on the roof of the car, he glared at her, too tired to be tactful. "A date, you mean? No. Even we 'sexy businessmen' need a night off occasionally."

"On a Friday night?"

He shrugged and opened the driver's-side door.

Before he could blink twice she scooted around to the passenger side and pulled open the door. "Mind if I come with you? If you're not busy tonight, this would be the ideal time to get to know the real you."

Damn those automatic door locks, anyway. If his car had the ordinary manual kind, the passenger door would still have been locked.

"I don't know," he said, stalling for time. "I'm awfully tired and had planned a quiet evening at home, maybe watch a movie."

"Great! I love movies." With a smug grin, she settled into the passenger seat, stowing at her feet the oversized tote she'd retrieved from the receptionist. "Aren't you getting in?"

Slowly, not finding any other recourse, he did so. "What about your car?"

A blithe wave dismissed his concern. "Oh, I came by taxi. I didn't have time to rent a car earlier because my plane was late. I'll just call a cab when we're done."

It figured.

He drove slowly out of the parking lot, still trying to find a way to ditch this leechlike interviewer. "I thought I'd rent a video, make some popcorn. Is that all right with you?" God, it sounded boring, even to him. Maybe all this bland domesticity would convince her—

"Sounds great. What kind of movies do you like?"

He mumbled a noncommittal answer, which she ignored as she launched into a cheery, one-sided conversation. He was still trying to come up with another plan when they arrived at the Video Palace.

The courtesy his mother had drilled into him made him ask, "Would you like to select something to watch?" then immediately regret the offer, fearing she'd take him up on it. Probably she'd pick one of those "chick" movies. He'd had far too rough a day to look forward to the likes of *Sleepless Magnolias of Endearment*!

But she surprised him. "You pick something out. After all, I can hardly learn anything about you if you're busy catering to my tastes, can I?"

Once inside the video store, he wandered around the aisles. This late on a Friday all the good stuff was already long gone. He'd wanted to see Bruce Willis's latest action release, but all the copies were rented. Ditto with Arnold Schwarzenegger's adventure movie and Denzel Washington's thriller.

In fact, the only titles remaining on the current-release shelves were chick flicks. Phooey.

Time to head over to the sci-fi section. Maybe an Ed Wood classic like *Plan 9 from Outer Space* would send C.J. running for the door. But halfway there, he stopped dead in his tracks. Slowly, he picked up the video that had caught his eye and stared at the movie's slipcase in fascinated glee. If ever there was a movie guaranteed to prove that he was the blandest, most boring person on the face of the earth, this was it.

A huge grin spreading over his face, he

grabbed a package of microwave popcorn and headed for the checkout. Mr. Dull-and-Worthy was back.

With a vengeance.

C.J. followed Jason into his comfortable Rancho Santa Fe home set atop a large, hilly lot. Since the stop at the video store, the oh-so-courteous, oh-so-bland demeanor he'd assumed just before the fire had returned. Once again, she was beginning to wonder if the man had a serious problem with split personalities, oscillating between his own version of Jekyll and Hyde.

If so, she really preferred the sexy-but-predatory Hyde.

"Make yourself at home." He waved her into an inviting and cozy den.

While obviously inhabited by a male—no female she knew would scatter the latest issues of *Sports Illustrated* and *Baseball News* with quite such abandon across the sturdy teak-and-tile coffee table—the room was surprisingly tidy. No stinky athletic socks lay strewn on the floor. No stray beer cans or overflowing ashtrays. In fact, except for the sports magazines, no clutter at all, and a faint aroma of potpourri tinged the air.

She sank her fingers into the back of a honey-colored leather overstuffed sofa with a subdued sigh. Trust a man to pick out super-comfortable furniture. "This is very pleasant. Did you decorate it yourself?"

"No. Can I get you something to drink? Iced tea? Coffee? Juice? Milk?"

Still more one-word answers. Continuing to chip away at his stone wall, she said agreeably, "Whatever you're having is fine." She watched him work in the kitchen area. "Uh, don't you drink?"

"Me? Oh, sure. See?" Triumphantly, he held up a glass of iced tea.

This was definitely frustrating. He was back to his Mr. Clean persona. With the crisis over and her journalistic instincts flaring, this could be the perfect moment to delve into his true personality—if only she could get him to loosen up a bit.

She wandered to the breakfast bar separating the kitchen from the den and leaned against a stool. "So what movie did you rent?"

An odd gleam appeared in his eyes. "One of my favorites. A classic. I'm sure you'll like it." He passed a glass of iced tea across the counter and stuck a packet of popcorn into the microwave. "I guess you're one of the magazine's best writers, huh? Did you always want to write?"

She sipped the tea. "I don't know. Maybe. It's something I can do well and it gives me a lot of freedom to travel."

"You like to travel?"

Poppety-pops from the microwave quickened

to a staccato beat. "Sure. I'm the original vaga-bond. My jobs have taken me all over the coun-try—you know, have laptop, will travel? And with a little luck—" She shut her mouth with a snap. How had she come so close to telling him about her pending job offer from *International Life*?

"With a little luck . . . ?" he prompted.

Casually, she shrugged. "Nothing really. Ex-cept that I'd like to see the world. Europe. Aus-tralia. The Orient." To distract herself as much as him, she dug into her purse and pulled out a passport, gleaming navy blue in its pristine cover. "See? I'm all set. Someday soon maybe I'll have the chance to use this." She briefly drifted into long-cherished dreams. "Maybe Japan first. Or Nepal. Katmandu—isn't the very name excit-ing?" She put the passport on the counter, where it fell open at the middle staple, revealing all too clearly the stampless freshness of unused pages.

He glanced down at the document, obviously noting its lack of ink and stamps. His hazel eyes, no longer analytical and dispassionate, shifted to her face, snaring her gaze.

"Sure," he said, nudging the booklet toward her with one long finger. "Very exciting."

Unwilling to answer the questions in his eyes, she glanced down and reached for the passport, but he picked it up with a quick grin and an unexpected mood change.

"Is your passport photo as bad as the ones they put on driver's licenses? Let me see."

But she snatched it away before he could look. "It's worse. Trust me."

"Darn! Here I thought I'd find out what C.J. stands for." The popcorn's snapping beat slowed to an occasional eruption. He gingerly took the puffy bag out of the oven and emptied it into a bowl. "What does it stand for, anyway?"

Responding to his lightened mood, she smiled. "That's for me to know and you—"

"To find out?"

"Nope. For you *not* to know."

Circling the breakfast bar with the bowl of steaming popcorn and their iced teas on a tray, he headed for the couch. "You realize you've challenged me, don't you? Now I'm going to have to find out for myself."

"Guess away," she said. C.J. settled herself beside him on the sofa, but a discreet two and a half feet away, with the giant bowl of popcorn nestled between them. "You'll never figure it out."

"I suppose Carolyn Jane is too obvious, huh?"

She nodded, her mouth full. "Much," she mumbled around her popcorn. Surprisingly, she was enjoying his company. He seemed to have transformed again, not into the super-sexy Hyde or the geeky Jekyll, but into someone else entirely. Someone warm and concerned and . . .

Stop it! You have no business liking him so much! Sternly, she lectured herself into obedience and determined to turn the subject away from herself and back to him. Wasn't that why she was here?

She looked around the spacious room, desperate for a new topic. "This seems like a big place for just one person." *How trite could she be?* Still, it was better than letting him continue his friendly interrogation.

"Well, Sam fills some of the space. We rub along pretty well together."

Sam? *Sam?*

Oh, God. He had a male roommate—was he gay? No wonder he seemed so . . . wait a minute. The occasional gleam in his eye had seemed to indicate . . . and what was that scene with his secretary . . . and how had this gotten past the magazine's editors . . . and . . .

Questions whirled through her mind faster than her boss pounced on expense-account reports, and with as little effect.

Meanwhile, Jason continued his guessing game, unaware of—or ignoring?—the shock that froze her in place. "Cleopatra Josephine? Clementine Jeanette? Carolyn Jewel? Christine—Sam!"

Sam?

Before she could ask, a gray-furred body plopped onto the coffee table. The animal reached into the bowl with one dexterous paw and neatly scooped out a kernel of popcorn. C.J. hastily jerked her hand back, wary of the feline sneak thief.

"Sam! Where are your manners?"

"Mrrrow!" Another neat swipe netted a second kernel of corn.

"C.J., meet my roommate, Sam." With a rueful shrug, Jason indicated the munching cat. "He keeps me company, gets me into trouble, and generally harasses me more than anyone else." He munched contemplatively for a moment before adding, "Except Rome. Maybe."

"He's a cat! But I thought—" Hastily, she shut her mouth before she admitted how high she'd jumped to arrive at her conclusion.

A quizzical gleam lit Jason's eyes, but he answered calmly enough. "Sure. *Felis catus*—or something. But don't tell him that, okay? I never told him he was adopted, so"—his voice dropped confidentially—"he won't believe you."

C.J. buried her nose in her iced tea to hide the heat that scorched her cheeks.

"Are you ready to watch the movie?" Jason asked after a brief, wary silence.

"Sure," she agreed.

He got up, put the tape he'd rented in the VCR, and sat down again, dislodging the bowl. By the time C.J. had rescued the bowl from the dual dangers of a near spill and the predatory cat, Jason had settled himself again—a mere foot from her. The bowl no longer fit between them.

She had no recourse but to set it on the coffee table.

And to try not to notice that her right side seemed to be glowing from the heat radiating from Jason's body.

"Hand me the remote, will you? It's in the drawer of that end table next to you."

She passed the elaborate device to him and pointed to a second one mounted on a small stand at his end of the coffee table. "What's wrong with the remote right there?" she asked curiously. "Or does it control something else?"

"Oh, that's Sam's remote. He likes to watch ESPN while I'm at work. The Cartoon Network too—Bugs Bunny is his hero." His voice was casual, distracted, while he flicked buttons on the device, turning on the large-screen television and tape player.

She stared at him. "Did you say that was Sam's? You mean the cat . . ." Surely she'd misheard him.

"Yeah, didn't you ever have a cat that watched TV? Sam learned how to work the remote control when he was about six months old. But he only knows what some of the buttons do. I was forever having to reset the system out of some weird state he'd somehow gotten it into. And sometimes he'd grab the control and change channels in the middle of a program. So, a year or so ago I got him a simple universal control of his own—one with big, easy-to-use buttons and not too many functions—and mounted it so he can reach it."

"I see." What other comment could she make to such an absurdity?

He grinned and grabbed another handful of popcorn. "Now we're both happy. He doesn't use my remote and I don't use his. He watches whatever he wants when I'm gone, and I watch what I want when I'm home. You have to compromise when you live with someone, you know."

C.J. eyed first Jason, then the cat, alertly standing—or rather sitting—guard by the popcorn bowl. For a brief moment she wondered what would happen if she made a sudden grab for more popcorn, then decided not to risk it.

"Tell me," she said in a deliberately chatty voice while keeping a wary eye on the cat, "do the scientists at the Salk Institute know about this miracle of feline intelligence?"

Jason's grin would have infuriated anyone who had less control over her emotions. "I take it you've never roomed with a cat?"

"No. My parents never let me have a pet." Not even after long, futile arguments that ended with a cold refusal and crushed feelings. With practiced skill, C.J. slammed those memories back into the corners of her mind.

"Ah. That explains it," Jason said with perfect seriousness. "The first thing you have to understand about owning a cat is that he isn't *your* pet—you're *his* pet."

"The cat is in charge. Right." She nodded with mock solemnity.

Jason grinned, punched a final button, and leaned back, plopping his sock-clad size-twelves on the table and ignoring her irony. "I'm glad to see you learn fast. It's a prime necessity in this household."

A flick of his wrist turned down the lamp at his end of the couch to a warm glow and the television erupted into life with a black-and-white trailer advertising a series of classic movie releases.

C.J., too, leaned back, only to discover that somehow Jason's arm had settled on the sofa back behind her shoulders. A casual gesture, surely. He wasn't even touching her, at least not really. Steeling herself to ignore the distraction, she said, "You never did tell me what we're going to watch."

His head turned and he looked down at her as he hit the pause button, freezing the screen. "Guess," he invited. "What kind of movie do you think I picked?"

Successfully grabbing a handful of popcorn without rousing the cat's ire, she chewed for a moment, then tapped her chin with buttery fingers. "Hmmm. I already know it's in black-and-white, so it's not a very recent release. Is it a

World War Two movie—something like *Destination Tokyo?*"

Jason shook his head no.

"Well, how about a Bogie-and-Bacall film, maybe *To Have and Have Not?*"

Another shake of his head, this time accompanied by a grin.

"I know. It's a monster movie, right? *The Wolf Man? The Mummy? Frankenstein?*"

"Nope."

What kind of movie *would* he pick? The silly question intrigued her. She wanted to know—badly—yet she also wanted to rise to the challenge of figuring it out for herself. Thinking back to all the other men of her acquaintance, she tried to fit what she knew of Jason into their molds—and failed. He simply didn't conform to the usual conventions.

What other man would buy his cat a remote control? What other man would have a cat in the first place? Animals could be troublesome and inconvenient—her parents had drummed that into her early. But Jason didn't seem worried by the demands his furry companion placed on him, nor was he threatened by admitting his affection for the animal, which now purred contentedly on the couch at his far side.

And she was almost sure he realized she'd thought him gay for a mad moment—yet he hadn't become offended or upset. Was he that secure in his own masculinity?

What kind of movie *had* he chosen?

Most men would choose a war movie or a detective story or a monster movie or even a western—that was it!

"I've got it! It's a western. Maybe *High Noon* or *Shane*. Something like that."

"Wrong again. Ready to see for yourself?"

Slowly, she nodded.

And sat stunned into immobility when the opening credits appeared.

THREE

"*It's a Wonderful Life*? That's your favorite movie?" The credits, announcing starring roles for Jimmy Stewart and Donna Reed, rolled past.

C.J.'s astonished question was balm to Jason's frustrated soul. The fire had fried his bland-and-dusty persona. He simply couldn't maintain a Mr. Dull disguise while dealing with frightened employees and a dangerous situation. And since C.J. was apparently intent upon sticking to his side with single-minded determination, his lapses into managerial proficiency had to have been noticed. Most likely, he had merely managed to confuse her.

Not to mention himself.

"Sure. Doesn't everyone like it?" he said, relishing her shock. A little confusion could only help. After all, confusion wasn't sexy—was it?

She stared at him as if he'd lost his mind. "I

don't think I've ever watched it, not all the way through, anyway. It's a bit, um, unsophisticated, isn't it?"

He hoped she misinterpreted his grin as anticipated pleasure in the film instead of satisfaction at getting back on his boring track. He'd seen the movie dozens of times—his mother had made it a Cooper family tradition at Christmastime—and knew it almost by heart. Someone like C.J. would surely find the simple heartwarming story boring.

He settled more comfortably, letting his arm droop slightly, and said mildly, "Well, you're in for a treat, then. Donna Reed is the sexiest lady in this movie."

"Donna Reed?" Her voice squeaked as she swiveled around to stare at him.

"Sure. Just watch." Firmly, he grasped her shoulder and turned her to face the big-screen TV opposite the couch.

Big mistake. His traitorous hand stuck to her and flatly refused to respond to the messages from his brain telling it to release her—now! Instead, his contrary fingers willfully started a slow, circular massage of her shoulder muscles that sent quivers of sensation from his fingertips to the nape of his neck, where they spiraled down his spine. She stiffened under the pressure, then relaxed, leaning ever so slightly in his direction.

Blindly, he stared at the screen, where two amorphous angels were discussing who would be sent down to Earth to answer the prayers of one George Bailey from the small town of Bedford Falls. In due time Clarence, an angel who had not yet earned his wings, was sent, despite having "the IQ of a rabbit."

"Sounds like some people I've worked with," C.J. muttered, tipping her head slightly toward Jason. A heady wave of sweet-musky perfume—gardenias and cinnamon?—drifted toward him and joined forces with the fire that coiled downward into his loins.

Sounds like me for being dumb enough to think this was a good idea. With firm resolve, he stopped his massage and forced his arm back onto the couch and away from the dangerous territory of her shoulders.

He cleared his throat. "Yes," he said, his voice still husky, "I know what you mean."

They watched in silence for a few minutes while George Bailey's early life played out on the screen. Jason gave far more attention to the rapid thumping of his heart and the elusive scent wafting from C.J.'s hair than to the movie. In the soft glow of the lamp, her nutmeg-brown hair glinted more amber than gold. He firmly suppressed the compelling urge to let his fingers stroke through the silky strands.

Watching this movie with her was a huge mistake, he realized. Instead of convincing her he wasn't the least bit sexy, he wanted more than anything for her to find him sexy as hell.

It's just testosterone, he assured himself.
How could it be anything more?

When James Stewart as George Bailey gave
up his college money to stay home and run the
family savings and loan company after his father's stroke, C.J. protested, "That's not fair! He
wanted to go off and see the world. Why should
he stay home?"

Personally, Jason had always sympathized
with the unfortunate George, but he had his
emotional impulses under firm control now. It
would do his case no good to agree with her.
Deliberately, he infused a note of self-righteous-
ness into his voice. "Maybe because it was the
right thing to do."

She whirled around to face him. "It can't be
right to give up your own dream for some ditzy
little company that you don't care about anyway."

Jason wasn't surprised by C.J.'s comment.
But given his private opinion that the movie was
more than a little sappy, he was surprised by his
urge to defend the fictional George. "The point
is George *does* care about the company and about
the town. It's his family."

"Family, hmmph! A bunch of millstones
around his neck, that's what they are. He wants
to be an architect, not some loan officer—and I'll
bet he'd be a good one too."

Jason scrounged the last bit of popcorn from
the annoyed Sam, then set the bowl aside. The

cat gave a protesting *mrrow!* and stalked out of the room to pout. "I take it you'd never have stayed home for the sake of your family."

"For *my* family? You must be kidding."

Sensing the pain hidden in her dismissive response, Jason couldn't resist probing further. "Why not? We all make sacrifices for family. It's the glue that holds us together."

"Not in my case. They wanted a whole lot more than I was willing to give. And when I refused, we came to a parting of the ways."

"You mean they kicked you out?"

C.J.'s lips pursed thoughtfully. "Not exactly. But they made it clear I was a sad disappointment to them, so I left."

Shocked, Jason tried to imagine a disagreement severe enough to have made his parents kick him—or his sister, Lyssa—out of the house. He couldn't think of one. "What happened?"

She shrugged, and he didn't think she was going to answer. But she finally said, "A lot of things really. Once I hit high school, it seemed like I was always on the outs with my parents. Then they wanted me to marry someone, the son of one of their friends. We got engaged, but I decided I didn't want to marry him after all. So I gave him the ring back and broke things off."

That couldn't be everything, could it? "And . . . ?"

She took a large swallow of iced tea. "And what?"

"You broke the engagement and what happened?" His gaze snared hers for a long moment, demanding an answer.

But her attention strayed to the television. "Did you see what George just did? How could he be so naive? Ten to one his brother never comes back home to take over the company." C.J.'s appalled comment was too obviously an effort to avoid Jason's question.

"I don't care what George just did. What happened when you broke your engagement?"

She gave a too casual shrug, her gaze still glued to the television. "I told my parents I didn't want to marry a guy who kissed like a fish."

"You mean you didn't love him?"

She tipped her head and considered it. "Yeah, basically." A long pause. "Anyway, my parents told me I had to. It was 'for my own good.' God! How I hate that phrase. They used it every time I didn't do what they wanted me to—which was often enough."

"So you refused to marry him anyway, right?"

"Right. We had a huge argument and I ended up walking out of the house. That's all."

Jason chewed that over in his mind while on the screen George Bailey got stuck with the savings and loan—again.

"So what did your parents say after you

cooled down and went back home? Did they give you a hard time?"

"I don't know. I never went back—did you see that dumb George try to make time with the blonde? Why would he think a girl like her wants sweet romance and a ride in the country? She's made for diamonds and good times."

Fed up with her constant attempts to distract him with George Bailey's pathetic life, Jason hit the pause button, freezing the picture with George Bailey in mid-stutter.

"What do you mean you never went back?" Jason demanded.

"What?" She still glared at the television.

Jason tugged her around to face him. "What do you mean you never went back home again?"

She glared at him, but he thought he saw a hint of pain lurking in the amber depths of her eyes. "Exactly what I said. I never went back. I called my parents, told them that I was moving out, and asked them to ship a suitcase of clothes to the YWCA. I haven't been back since."

Shock rippled down Jason's spine. "That's terrible. You've never seen your family again?"

She shrugged, and whether by accident or design, the movement dislodged her chin from his palm. "Oh, if I'm in town—they live in Houston—I give them a call, and a few times I've met my mother or sister for lunch somewhere. It's no real loss, truly. In their eyes I never did anything right while I was home, so my leaving was inevitable. The broken engagement was just the final straw. For all of us." Curiosity sparkled in her eyes. "Why are you so upset? It's no tragedy. I was nineteen, old enough to be out on my own."

"You were only *nineteen*?"

Jason couldn't keep still. Abruptly he pushed himself to his feet and stalked around the family room. He remembered his own youthful vulnerability at nineteen. He'd been only a sophomore in college at that age and so wet behind the ears that he'd practically dripped water wherever he went.

"What were your parents thinking of?" he finally asked.

"The financial benefits of allying themselves to Charles's family, I suppose," C.J. said tartly. "His father was one of the family company's biggest customers. But it all worked out fine. My younger sister Louise married Charles instead."

If anything, her blunt response appalled Jason all the more. What kind of parents would encourage—no, *demand*—that their daughter marry for money? Listening to her tell this sad tale was like peeling an onion—only now had he arrived at the inner-core truth. He'd been right in his first reaction: Her parents really had kicked her out—in spirit if not in fact.

But before he could delve any further, C.J. plunked her empty iced-tea glass onto the coffee table. "Why are we talking about me? I'm supposed to be finding out about you, remember?"

Well, hell. She was right. Her personal life was none of his business. Which did nothing to satisfy his inexplicable need to know more about her. He raked his hand through his hair, picked up both their glasses, and walked into the kitchen to refill them. Anything to keep himself from doing what his impulses urged him to do.

You're losing your grip, buddy. You're not supposed to be getting closer to C.J. She's the enemy, remember?

True enough, he conceded. He wanted to be rid of the writer, not get involved with her. Still, his heart ached at the thought of her as a lonely, vulnerable kid forced to look after herself at too young an age. And other parts of his body ached as much, as he remembered how she'd felt under his arm. His mind still reveled in her spicy-sweet fragrance, which jerked his body enough to spill a couple of ice cubes.

"Is everything okay in there?" She must have heard the clatter of the ice skittering over the countertop.

"Uh, sure. I'll just be a minute."

She's about as vulnerable as a lioness, his rational mind insisted. *Watch your step with her. You're supposed to be turning her off with your boring personality, not turning yourself on.*

"Easier said than done," he said under his breath. The memory of how right she'd felt under his hands prodded him into taking a deep, restorative breath.

"Did you say something?" C.J. called.

"I said, I'm almost done in here." How could he be so attracted to a woman so clearly unavailable, both because of her profession and because her personality was so obviously his opposite?

Yeah, but opposites sure as hell could attract.

When he returned to the family room, he had a firm grip on both the refilled glasses and his self-control. He was sure of only one thing: Under *no* circumstances would he let himself get close enough to her to be tempted again. Distance, that would do it.

With a precise clink, he set her glass down in front of her, making sure he stayed on the far side of the coffee table. To reinforce his decision, he stayed upright and leaned against the mantel. No point taking any chances. "What do you want to know?" he asked.

"Well, how about telling me why *It's a Wonderful Life* is your favorite movie."

An answer popped out before he had time to think about it. "It reminds me of our family Christmases. Every year my mother would find out when it was going to be on television and insist that we all gather around with homemade cookies and hot mulled cider to watch it. Sometimes, when I got older, I'd have a date over, but mostly it was just family—my parents and Lyssa and me and any grandparents or aunts and uncles who were in town."

The warmth of his memories made him smile. "Mom made these truly awful peanut-butter-surprise cookies every year. They tasted really bad, but they were so complicated to make, no one had the heart to tell her we all hated them. We gave her compliments galore each year on how much more delicious they tasted than the previous year's batch. So . . . she kept making them for us. It wasn't until she and Dad went off on a Peace Corps mission after Lyssa graduated from college and she was getting all weepy about not being home to make her peanut-butter-surprise cookies that year that we fessed up."

"Was she upset?"

He nodded, remembering his mother's surprised dismay. "Yeah, but then Dad pointed out that we'd all swallowed them without a murmur because we loved her and didn't want her to be disappointed or hurt."

There was a long silence while C.J. absorbed this. Finally she grinned and said, "You're just lucky she didn't make them for you at times other than Christmas."

He shot her a glance. Despite the smile, her voice seemed a bit husky, as if strained by something, but her bland expression gave no clue to her thoughts. "We had to do some fast talking a couple of times, but we finally convinced her that particular cookie recipe should be saved as a special holiday, um, 'treat.' "

Another pause, but this time he noticed her eyes blinking hard. Her face was tipped downward, so he couldn't see her expression. She prompted him with, "So the movie symbolizes . . . ?"

"Family. Love. Togetherness. All those things." To his surprise, he realized it *did* mean all those silly, tug-your-heart, sentimental notions. "To this day, Lyssa still rents the movie each Christmas and carries on the tradition with Jason and her kids. *Without* the peanut-butter-surprise cookies."

Maybe he'd stopped paying attention to the movie years ago, maybe he'd come to think the movie boring, but he realized he'd miss seeing it if Lyssa weren't still gathering the family at the holidays. Maybe there was more to this holiday-tradition stuff than he'd thought.

Yeah, that might explain why his hormones surged when he sat next to C.J. He'd just gotten swept up with too many memories of snuggling with girlfriends and family while watching Jimmy Stewart go through his paces.

Reflex, that's what it was. Just a simple conditioned reflex. Like Pavlov's dogs.

"What about your parents? Don't they continue to watch it with you?" Her face was still turned away from him, but that husky note in her voice was even stronger than before.

He laughed, in equal parts relief at finally understanding his reaction to C.J. and affectionate amusement at his parents' "retirement." "Sure they would—except they're on yet another Peace Corps mission at the moment. Mom and Dad are in Peru, having the time of their lives."

He waited for her next question, then took a long look at her. "You're crying! What's the matter?"

Her spine visibly stiffened and she cleared her throat before glaring at him. "I am not! I got something in my eye and it watered for a minute, that's all." As if to back up her claim, she carefully dabbed a finger across one eye.

"Oh." Not that he believed her for a moment. He noticed the frozen picture of Jimmy Stewart still caught in the blonde girl's jeering laughter and asked, "Do you want to continue with the movie?"

"Sure. Like I said, I don't think I've ever actually watched it all the way through. My family tended to avoid stuff that was, uh, sentimental."

He had a sudden image of her as a little girl trapped with parents too cold and too unloving to bother with simple, sweet traditions. Rage at their blindness licked through him, followed closely by a burning need to comfort that little girl. Without thinking, he sat next to C.J. on the couch and reached for the remote control.

Too close! You were supposed to keep your distance! You're too close!

All his senses screamed the warning as the heat from her body warmed his side. But if he was too close to her, it was also too late to move away. Caught in the sensual trap she unconsciously spun, and charged up with an urgent need to comfort her, he couldn't let her go. Instead, he deliberately placed his arm around her shoulders—not on the couch as before, but actually around her—propped his feet back on the coffee table, and pulled her against his side.

Lord, she felt right in his arms!

C.J. couldn't believe she was this comfortable leaning against Jason Cooper. Why didn't she pull away? Why didn't she tell him to go to hell? Why didn't she—

Aw, darn. Her body wasn't listening anyway. All her body wanted to do was sink farther into the warmth of him and revel in his protective embrace. With a sigh, she yielded to the urge that smothered her professional instincts and nestled closer against his side. Head tucked against his shoulder, she languidly reached out and pressed the play button on the remote he held.

The image on the screen began to move. For several minutes C.J. absently took in the figures moving and talking on the screen. But her attention was truly concentrated on the delicious sensations of Jason's hand idly caressing her waist, Jason's legs tangled with hers, Jason's chin nudging the crown of her head.

On the screen, George Bailey visited with Mary in her front parlor. C.J. smiled as she realized that Donna Reed, playing Mary, really did have a charming, innocent sensuality. Maybe it was because Mary was so clearly in love with the oblivious George.

Then her breath caught as Mary and George shared the telephone to talk to someone, their faces close together, their breaths warming each other's lips.

A sudden image of being that close to Jason blinded her to the pictures on the screen. She *was* almost that close. All he'd have to do was tilt his chin downward—just a little—while she tipped her face upward—just a little—and . . .

Under her ear, Jason's heart thudded. A flick of his fingers on the remote control stopped the film, then powered off the television. From the corner of her eye she saw the screen go blank, but didn't care. She was more engrossed in the sensations Jason ignited in her than in watching some old movie.

His hand shifted, moving up toward the side of her breast. She held her breath, waiting with high-wire tension for him to cover the fullness that strained toward his touch. When his other hand came up to her chin and tipped her head upward, she stared directly at his lips.

Luscious, utterly masculine lips. A finely carved upper lip. A lower lip with a sensitive fullness that lured her like nectar lured a hummingbird. Like that delicate, determined bird, she wanted to taste his kiss—just a sip, really, she assured herself. Not a *real* kiss. Just enough to find out if he tasted as delicious as he looked.

She lifted her gaze beyond his straight, strong nose to the shadowy hazel eyes, now glinting green in the lampglow.

She read a question in his eyes, one that made her pause for a long moment. His thumb curved over her chin and pressed her lips, tugging the lower one down slightly. The sweep-tug of the motion teased her mouth with torrid heat.

Hesitantly, she lifted her hand to his cheek. Tracing the outline of his face, she delicately ran her finger over his eyebrows, down his cheek-bone, right to the edge of that far-too-tempting mouth. Her finger mimicked the action of his thumb. His warm breath caressed her hand with sensual heat.

He opened his mouth slightly and drew her forefinger inside. His tongue and teeth nipped and nibbled and teased the finger, just as his thumb probed for entrance to her mouth. She yielded to his silent request, letting her own mouth open to draw his thumb inside.

He tasted wonderful. Spicy. Tempting. *Manly*. But the almost innocent exchange between lips and fingers suddenly wasn't enough. She wanted more—the taste of his mouth on her tongue, the heat of his lips against hers.

With a sigh that emanated from somewhere

down around her toes and with his willing help, she shifted her body over his. In seconds she was pressed against him from head to toe, her arms holding him close, her breasts pressed against his chest.

And he stole her breath with his kiss.

FOUR

Somewhere in the tangle of tongues and lips Jason forgot what he was supposed to do. He forgot to be bland and inoffensive. He forgot to convince C.J. that he wasn't the least bit sexy. He forgot—he even forgot what it was he'd forgotten.

Instead, the silken moisture of C.J.'s lips snared his attention. As did the gentle heat his tongue discovered on her mouth. As did the texture of her fingertips rubbing against his cheek. As did her humid breath tingling across his face.

As she *did.*

Startled by the realization, he pulled away from her for three ragged heartbeats. What was he—what were they—doing? With a finger he had to concentrate to steady, he outlined the curve of her lips. All he'd intended was to—what?

He didn't know. "C.J.—" he began, then didn't know what to add.

Her long lashes, improbably lush and full, swept up to reveal eyes the color of cinnamon toast. "What?" Her voice was soft, throaty.

He shook his head, already losing the thought. "Nothing. Just . . . C.J." Deliberately he held her gaze while he lowered his head slowly to hers. His hand, curling around her waist, inched upward, finding the swell of her breast at the same instant as his mouth took possession of hers.

C.J. barely knew which action was more devastating, Jason's firm control of her mouth or his hand's gentle cupping of her breast. It didn't matter because her own hands framed his face, keeping his lips locked to hers. He tasted so good, she thought fuzzily. Like dark, rich chocolate, sinful and delicious—and utterly seductive.

A simple kiss, a mere touching of lips, exploded into deep, searching probes that ravished her concentration. Her mouth opened in silent invitation to his tongue's exploration. He didn't hesitate to accept. Through her silk blouse and bra, his fingers plucked the peaking crown of her breast and sent rivers of delight coursing through her.

When he tore his lips from hers she started to protest, then let the complaint dissolve into a satisfied sigh as his mouth trailed across her cheek and down the sensitive skin of her neck.

Shivers rippled from each press of his lips against her skin. She clutched his head, not so much to guide him to more sensitive areas—every place he touched was hypersensitive—but to ensure he didn't move away from her any farther than the space needed to take a breath.

Her own breath came in deep pants that echoed the pace of his. Vaguely, she wondered when she'd lost control of things. Had it been when he'd caressed her breast? Or when his tongue stroked her mouth? Or when he'd outlined her lips with his thumb?

Or when she'd rolled on top of him?

When *she'd* rolled on top of *him*?

Oh, no! She'd started this. What had happened to her businesslike demeanor?

She pulled back abruptly, jerking herself away from him so quickly that he let out a startled "oof!"

"What's wrong?"

"What's right would be a better question," she snapped, rolling away from him and staggering to her feet. She almost tripped, but managed to catch her balance before he could touch her to help.

Shakily, she speared her hand through her hair. It had started so innocently, watching a movie that would make a Bugs Bunny cartoon look like adult entertainment. When had things spiraled out of control?

She walked to the fireplace and gripped the

mantel with both hands. When she thought she could control her voice, she asked, "What was that about?"

"What was *what* about?"

A bit more certain of her self-control, she released the mantel and turned to face Jason—and immediately recognized her mistake. He sat on the couch, leaning forward, with his elbows propped on his knees. Frustrated desire sparked his hazel eyes with green glints. With his hair tousled and the neckline of his knit shirt completely undone, he looked as tempting as a giant box of Godiva chocolates and twice as hazardous to her health. Chocolates only endangered her waistline, while Jason Cooper endangered her . . .

Not quite daring to complete that thought, she focused on the shadowy vee of his chest that peeped out through the shirt. She tightened her hands into fists to subdue the urge to run her fingers over the rest of the bronzed chest that lay beneath the shirt.

"Well?" His impatient question jerked her attention back to the real issue.

"Well what?"

"What's going on with you? Why the sudden retreat?"

She tipped her chin upward with more defiance than she felt. "We'd gone far enough. I was just calling a halt to something that never should have gotten started."

"Why not? We're both adults. We're both free to—" He eyed her with sudden suspicion. "Is that it? Are you involved with someone else?"

"It has nothing to do with any other relationships I may or may not have," she began, only to be interrupted.

He surged to his feet. "Like hell it doesn't. Are you married?"

Surprised, she answered before she even thought to protest. "No!"

"Engaged?"

"No."

"Living with someone?"

"Of course not."

"Seriously involved with someone?"

She shook her head.

The breath he took surely wasn't one of relief. "Good. Neither am I—for any of the above. So why did you call things off just as they were getting interesting?"

When had he moved to stand right beside her? She had to lean her head back to look directly into his eyes. "They were getting *too* interesting. I didn't come here for that." Her gesture at the couch explained which "that" she meant.

Miraculously, his expression softened. His hand stroked her cheek. "I know you didn't, sugar. I didn't plan it either. We're just a bit too . . . combustible, I guess."

Stiffening her spine to generate some confidence, she stepped away from him. "I'm not going to get involved with you, Jason," she told him bluntly. "It's unprofessional—and I'm never unprofessional."

He angled his head to the side, as if seriously considering her argument. "It would only be unprofessional if you let it interfere with your work—and you'd never do that, would you?"

"Of course not!"

He nodded. "That's what I thought. I wouldn't either. So why not explore the fire? There's something sizzling in here, and I refuse to believe I'm the only one burning."

Some instinct for self-preservation insisted that she keep her mouth shut about the presence of any such sizzle—imaginary or not. Instead, she infused calm into her voice. "I'm not going to explore anything further with you, no matter how persuasive you are—and you're very persuasive, aren't you? You know," she added thoughtfully, "I'm finally beginning to understand why my editor picked you as California's sexiest businessman."

That stopped him cold. To her surprise, he rubbed his face with his hand and muttered a low curse. "I'd forgotten about that."

Her curiosity took control of her tongue. "Tell me something. Why were you dressed so, um, oddly when I first arrived at your office?"

"Oddly?" Wariness clouded his face.

"You know. Like you were chief gerbil or something."

He choked on a laugh. "Cora Greene called me a hamster."

"Hamster, gerbil, whatever. Why were you dressed like that?"

He paced once around the room, obviously debating his next words. Finally, he stopped right in front of her and took a deep breath. "I have something to confess."

"I'm listening."

Jason's struggle to find just the right words was obvious. "Earlier, when you arrived, I had, um, modified my appearance. I don't usually dress like a . . ."

"Hamster?"

He shot C.J. a glare, but nodded. "Yeah. I wanted to make an impression on you."

"So you dressed up like a rodent?" she asked incredulously. "Some impression."

"Look, I was trying to make a *specific* impression. And I thought dressing that way would do it."

"Okay. What impression? And why?"

"That's the hard part," he muttered, then finally admitted, "I just wanted you to change your mind about profiling me for your magazine."

She stared at him. "But you agreed to the interview."

"No, I didn't. Rome agreed to it, not me. See, he was picked a few years ago, and it was great for business. So a few weeks ago, when your editor approached him about profiling me, he thought it would be a good idea."

"I see." C.J. tapped her chin with her finger. "So he signed you up to be California's sexiest businessman without your consent. How does that explain the rodent disguise?"

"I know about the recent purchase of *California Business* by Solomon Mooney."

"So?" She tried to stifle the instant flush of guilt that burned her cheeks. Jason couldn't possibly know about the memo resting in her briefcase. The new owner had very . . . interesting ideas on how to write personal-profile articles. When her editor had handed the memo to her as she was leaving the office, she'd almost tossed it back at him. Then she remembered that in her new job at *International Living*—another Mooney publication—she'd be writing the same kind of scandal-mongering articles. She might as well practice on Jason Cooper, she'd thought.

Until now.

"So what?" she asked again.

"So I don't want my life turned into a sideshow attraction. I've been there, done that. And I didn't like it."

Her curiosity couldn't resist that opening. "What does that mean?"

He stared at her from under lowered brows, then relaxed slightly. "I guess there's no harm in telling you. A few years ago I was dating a girl I'd known since high school—since junior high, actually. She'd become quite successful on her own—"

"As what?" C.J. interrupted.

"As a model. She signed with the Ford Agency and was on the covers of magazines all the time. Even got a stint doing swimsuits for *Sports Illustrated.* Anyway, someone in the tabloids heard that she was having some personal problems. It was all the stress—that, and never having thirty seconds to call her own. She used to come over here, more to get away from people than anything else. The paparazzi hounded her—and me—for months. Hell, they had us engaged, married, and with two kids on the way every time we called out for pizza!"

She pondered this information, then asked, "What happened?"

His gaze met hers and she saw the bleakness chilling the hazel of his eyes to a flat brown. "About what you might expect. She lost control of herself, got hooked on booze and some prescription drugs, and had to check into a rehab clinic. By the time she came out, she was twenty pounds heavier and there was some other new face headed for superstardom—and her career was ruined."

After a moment C.J. murmured, "I'm sorry."

"Yeah, me too. She's a nice person. She's a real-estate agent these days and finally getting her life on track. Though she still has a bit of a problem with public appearances."

C.J. hardened her sensibilities. "I can see why you're not enthusiastic, but aren't you panicking over nothing? I doubt if one little article about you would send you hiding under a tequila bottle. Besides, why didn't you just contact my editor and cancel?"

"Well, that's the embarrassing part. I didn't find out you were coming until this morning." He stalked over to the fireplace, turned, and glowered at her. "I suspect Rome and Cora conspired to keep me from finding out until it was too late."

Thinking of the intimidating Cora Greene and her way of combining maternal care with a dictator's commands, C.J. had to admit that it was possible Jason was right. That also explained Cora's frantic fussing with Jason's appearance when she'd arrived.

"So you got blindsided, as it were." She thought a moment, then added, "But I'm still surprised you don't want to be publicly acknowledged as the sexiest businessman in California. Most guys would line up for the privilege."

"I saw what happened to Rome when his profile was published. Women were everywhere—he had no privacy at all. One even convinced his housekeeper that she was Rome's date and was catering his dinner. The woman had a seven-course meal waiting for him when he came home."

"What's so bad about that?"

"She served it in the nude!" he told her, outrage ringing in his tone. "He'd brought a lady friend home and there this other person was, stark naked and draped over his couch!"

C.J. tried, but couldn't stifle a giggle. "Sounds like the average male's fantasy date. And it didn't cost him a cent."

"Maybe so, but the profile that was published had a little mistake in it. It said Rome loved shellfish. Actually, he's allergic to them. And every single dish the naked woman prepared had some form of shellfish in it—even dessert! The woman kept shoving food in his face, and when he finally swallowed a bite just to get her to back off, he immediately broke out in hives. He spent the rest of the night in the emergency room."

By now Jason was pacing through the family room like an impatient father-to-be.

C.J.'s laughter welled up before she could stop it. Through her chuckles she said, "I promise I'll double-check to make sure I get the facts straight, all right? Will that satisfy you?"

He stopped in front of her. "No! I don't want to be profiled at all. Don't you see, I'm just an average guy, not some hot dude who needs an armful of women to stroke his ego. I don't want to be treated like some brainless boy toy just to give the business a shot in the arm."

He was serious! For the first time C.J. realized that this assignment might turn into her first professional failure. Images of calling the editor and explaining that California's sexiest business-man had declined the honor sent a shiver down C.J.'s spine. No way did she want to leave on that kind of a note. No, she wanted the editor to be so impressed by her work that he'd be pining for her return. *Always leave 'em wanting more.*

She had to convince Jason to continue with the profile. Surely there was something she could offer him that would get him to cooperate.

"So you're worried about getting the tabloid treatment if you let me go on with the project?" she asked slowly, trying to nail down his ultimate objection.

"That's part of it, yeah."

"What if I promise to let you read the article before I submit it? Would that reassure you?" When he hesitated, she added, "Believe me, this isn't an offer I make lightly—or often."

"Why can't you just find someone else to persecute?" he asked stubbornly. "Why does it have to be me?"

"Well, actually, you were third on the list this year," she admitted. "The first-choice guy just got married last month—and married men are out for obvious reasons. And the second guy . . ." Her words trailed off.

"What's wrong with him?"

"He just came out of the closet. He's gay." She shrugged. "Obviously *not* a good choice to appeal to female readers. Which is, by the way, the entire point of the series. *California Business* is trying to increase its readership with women. Featuring a sexy guy is a great selling point."

"But I'm not all *that* sexy," he protested.

For some reason, her gaze instantly zeroed in on that honey leather sofa where she had been lip-locked with Jason. A slow burn rose up her neck and across her face. Defying her own embarrassment, she met his gaze. "You couldn't have proved that by me ten minutes ago."

When a matching dark red flush rose in his face, she knew he'd caught her meaning. "Damn! I didn't intend for that to happen, you know."

She nodded her acceptance. "I know. Neither did I. It's all right. We'll just have to be more professional from now on."

"You're assuming there's a 'from now on' to worry about. I don't think we've come to a firm agreement about that—yet."

"I offered to let you see what I write about you before it's submitted."

Jason studied her so intently she wanted to squirm, but she forced herself to meet his gaze steadily and without flinching.

"All right," he said at last. "If you let me see the article first, I'll let you tag along the rest of the week. But I warn you, I'm not going out of my way to make myself look like anything except what I am. Deal?"

"Deal." She offered a confirming handshake.

He took her hand, then hesitated until she was half-convinced he would pull her into his arms and kiss her. If he did, she tried to convince herself that she'd be outraged.

With his gaze focused on her mouth and those telltale green sparks lighting his eyes, every nerve inside her quivered in anticipation. But he didn't kiss her. Instead, he gave her hand an impersonal shake, and released it. Meanwhile, she concentrated on shoring up knees that seemed determined to disintegrate into overcooked pasta.

"I guess that's it," she said, curling her fingers to shield the last vestiges of his touch.

"Yeah. I guess it is."

She had to get out of there before she threw herself at him and begged him to finish what he'd started on that sofa. "Sure. Okay. Could you call me a cab? My plane was late and I don't have a rental car yet."

"That's all right. I'll take you to your hotel." Almost as if he was relieved to have something specific to do, Jason turned away and collected his keys. "Where are you staying?" he asked as he led the way to the door.

"Well, actually, I don't have a hotel room yet either," she admitted.

He stopped dead and turned to look at her with a razor-sharp gaze. "You don't have a place to stay?"

She shook her head. "Not exactly."

He rubbed a hand over his face and studied the clock on the wall, now pointing to ten minutes past ten. "According to the paper, there are five major conventions in town this weekend."

She nodded.

"You didn't have a reservation anywhere?"

"Well, I had one. It wasn't guaranteed for late arrival—I was supposed to check in before coming to see you. Then the plane was late and there was the fire. . . ." She paused, then added the final blow. "The reservations desk warned me that the hotel was overbooked already, but I'm sure they'll find someplace for me to sleep."

With a resigned sigh, he tossed his keys back onto the counter.

"Hell. I guess that means you're staying here."

Jason pounded his pillow into a new, equally uncomfortable state, and tugged ineffectually at the sheet. Just down the hall, C.J. was no doubt sleeping peacefully while he lay here tossing and turning. After two more futile attempts to make himself comfortable, he got out of bed and walked to the window.

He'd had lots of overnight guests before— acquaintances looking for a place to crash while they saw San Diego's sights, college buddies in town for a day or two, even once or twice a friend of Lyssa's who needed an emergency bed for the night. It happened all the time to anyone who lived in a vacation destination and who was foolish enough to have a spare bedroom. A woman sleeping down the hall—he'd carefully given her the bedroom farthest from his own—shouldn't be that big a deal.

But he'd never had an overnight guest whom he wanted as badly as he wanted C.J.

The ache in his groin felt permanent, even though he knew only a few hours had passed. He never should have watched that damned movie—or *any* movie—with her. Sitting with her cuddled against him was too much to ask of any man. He should have known he was setting himself up for torture.

It was just propinquity. Hell, Rome would never let him live it down if he discovered that C.J. turned him on like this. All he had to do was remember that his current state of arousal was strictly a normal hormonal reaction he'd have had to any attractive woman and he'd be okay.

He'd almost convinced himself of that when he remembered her warm brown hair glinting in the lamplight. The silky stuff had smelled vaguely of apples and spice. And her lips tasted of the same summer-cider sunshine. His arousal stiffened to new heights.

He had to get himself under control. Determinedly, he headed for the bathroom. A cold shower might help him gain a little perspective. At the very least it would give him something different to groan over.

But even with frigid water beating against his skin, his mind kept replaying those moments on the couch, when he'd held her and she'd responded with a warm passion that contradicted everything he sensed about her.

It's all my imagination. She's not really that passionate. I'm not really that attracted to her. It's just imagination. Hormones. Propinquity.

Desire.

He stepped out of the shower and toweled himself dry. Even with goose bumps pebbling his skin, his arousal was undaunted. Stoically, he turned the shower on again and resigned himself to yet another dousing of icy water.

Tomorrow, by heaven, he would find a way to keep things cool between them. Tomorrow he would maintain a calm, professional distance between himself and C.J. She'd never do this to him again. She'd get her article, and he'd make sure it didn't say one damned thing he didn't approve of. And then she'd go away and he'd never see her again.

His life would be back under control. Cora would bow to his every whim. Rome would get his comeuppance in some gleefully unanticipated way. As for him, he'd be cool. Calm. Professional.

Lonely.

The phone rang early Saturday morning, demanding attention. Up since sunrise, Jason stalked inside and grabbed the cordless.

"Yeah," he growled. He stomped his way back to the driveway. A near-sleepless night interrupted by intermittent cold showers had done nothing positive for his mood.

"Hey, buddy, it's me, Rome."

"Fine time of the morning to be calling. It's barely seven o'clock."

"I figured you'd be up. Uh, you *were* up, weren't you?"

In more ways than one, Jason thought, remembering his persistent, nightlong arousal that even now had only half abated. "What do you want?"

"Just thought I'd tell you that you did good yesterday. I'm at the warehouse now. The damage is minimal—mostly in the attic and air-conditioning system. With luck and some cooperation from a couple of contractors I know, we'll be back on track by Monday."

"Good."

Naturally Rome ignored the implied why-don't-you-hang-up-now. "So what's eating you?"

"Nothing."

"Sure. And I'm planning to paint the warehouse purple and green. With orange stripes."

"Should do a lot to improve morale."

Rome sighed audibly. "C'mon, buddy. Spill it. What's wrong?"

"It's that damned writer. C. J. Stone."

The silence deafened Jason as he lodged the phone between his hunched shoulder and ear and uncoiled the garden hose from its holder.

Finally Rome asked, "What about her? Is she being, uh, too intrusive?"

"Only if you think it's too intrusive to park herself in my guest room." The instant the words popped out, Jason wanted to smack himself upside the head. He never meant to admit that much, even to his best friend.

"She slept over last night?" Jason heard a noise as Rome hastily slammed a door, cutting off the vague mutter of voices and movement in the background. "Jase, are you out of your ever-lovin' mind?"

"Probably. But didn't you hear what I said? She stayed in the guest room, not my bedroom."

"So you're claiming you never do it except in your own bed? C'mon, Jase, this is me, Rome. Get real."

Jason's jaw ached from the effort to spit out the words. "I'm telling you she slept in the guest room. *Alone.*"

Another long silence while Jason guided the hose toward the car waiting in the driveway for its weekly wash. Normally, the chore was a pleasant, mind-numbing one that soothed and relaxed him. Today he suspected that the task would be less than effective as a tranquilizer.

"All right. If you say you're not involved with her, I'll believe it." Rome's tone indicated he certainly didn't believe it. "So how did the lady writer end up at your place?"

Jason paused, a bucket and sponge in one hand. "God's honest truth, Rome, I have no idea. She just . . . happened, I guess. We were watching a movie and—" Abruptly, he slammed his jaw shut. No need to go into what he privately termed That Kiss.

"She's good, I'll say that for her," Rome said, after waiting in vain for Jason to complete his explanation.

Good? She's mind-blowing. Incredible. Sexier than a brand new 'Vette and twice as dangerous. Without trying, Jason invoked the memory of every texture and sensation from That Kiss in far too vivid detail. But he sure as hell resented Rome offering such an intimate opinion of C.J. And he didn't want anyone—anyone *else*—speculating on C.J.'s talents, in bed or out. Rome better get that straight right now. "She's a professional writer, okay? She—*we*—didn't do anything last night except work on the article. Got it?"

"Uh—got it."

Jason plopped a plastic bottle of car cleaner onto the brick driveway beside the half-filled bucket of water and listened hard for any trace of sarcasm or disbelief in Rome's agreement. To his relief, he heard none, though he might have imagined that thread of humor in Rome's voice.

"So tell me why else you called," Jason said, determined to change the subject.

This time he was sure he heard a chuckle. "Lyssa has declared tonight as Mom's Night Off, and I've promised to take her to that new seafood restaurant in Del Mar. I've decided to give you first crack at looking after the Terrible Trio."

Good humor immediately restored, Jason chuckled. "First crack, huh? Does this mean I'll be subjected to torture by tiny tots? Exhausted by energetic imps? Run ragged by wrestling rugrats?"

"Yup. That's about the size of it." Rome paused. "Of course, if you'd rather I call a regular baby-sitter . . ."

"Over your dead body! I'll be happy to handle the critters for you. 'Bout time you learned how a master does it anyway."

"Ri-ight. I'll take notes—if you survive. Um, why not bring your houseguest with you? It'll do her good to see you in your natural state, on the floor playing with toys. Give her a whole new perspective on you, if you know what I mean."

"Yeah," Jason agreed slowly, staring up at the second-floor window of the room where C.J. had slept. He could envision her all too clearly, lying in rumpled disarray, her dark hair spread over the pillow, her leg half-revealed in the golden morning sunlight. Hell, he didn't even have to see her to send his imagination flying to new heights. He wanted to know what she wore to bed in the worst way. A filmy negligee? A flannel granny gown? A T-shirt and panties? Or maybe, possibly, nothing but her own peaches-and-cream skin?

When a spurt of cold water squirted across his sneakers, he jerked his gaze away from that window. He'd practically strangled the sponge thinking about C.J.'s sleeping garments. Disgusted, he slam-dunked the sponge into the bucket, sending water spraying in all directions. He forced his attention back on Rome's voice.

Rome might be right in thinking that bringing C.J. with him was a good idea, he admitted silently while he finalized the baby-sitting arrangements. He wanted C.J. to know him as a person, not as some studly sex object—at least, he wanted her to know him as a person too. So, seeing him interact with his family might be a perfect way for him to get past the barriers she'd thrown up last night. And he never passed up an opportunity to be with the kids.

Besides, looking after three active toddlers might be almost enough distraction to keep his mind—and his hands—off a woman far too disturbing to be trusted.

FIVE

C.J. lay in bed, trying to get the nerve to face the day. Through the barely open window, sounds drifted up from outside. Jason must already be up and out, fiddling with something just below her window. A glance at the clock showed the hands creeping closer to the seven-fifteen mark. Time to get up.

Time to face him.

Ugh. Where had that nasty thought come from? She kicked off the covers and forced herself out of bed. She had to face the day—and Jason—sometime, and better now than never. Heading for the attached bath, she reviewed her plans by producing her habitual mental to-do list.

Do an in-depth interview with Jason Cooper. Check.

Rebuild her cool, in-control persona. Check.

Make sure that no further lapses in professionalism occur. Check.

Do *not* kiss the man, no matter how tempting the situation.

She further refined the list as she showered and dressed in a pair of designer jeans and a classic-but-comfortable silk blouse. Jason might be having a weekend off, but she was still on duty. Besides, a little makeup and an I'm-here-to-work outfit would give her the confidence to face down even California's sexiest businessman. With luck, her denim-and-silk uniform would keep her mind on business even though she'd kissed him senseless last night. Or been kissed senseless. Whichever.

Before she could decide, a strident electronic chirp sounded. C.J. dug out her cell phone and answered warily. The list of people who had her number was too short for this not to be important.

"Ceej! Glad I caught you." Walter Bates, editor for *California Business*, sounded as cheery as if he'd been chomping unwary writers for breakfast.

She hated the way he slurred "C.J." to make "Ceej." In retaliation, she shortened the editor's name into a nickname she knew he hated. "What's up, Wally?" Whatever it was couldn't be good.

"Oh, not much. Just wanted to check in and

see how your interview with Jesse Hooper is going."

This he needed to know on a Saturday morning? Right. Something was *definitely* cooking.
"That's Jason Cooper," she said, enunciating
carefully, "and everything's fine. Got a great picture or two of him yesterday, in fact. Maybe
cover quality. Why?"

A thrum-te-thum echoed over the phone
link. Wally was drumming his fingers on something hard. C.J. waited for the ax to fall.

"Good. Good. About your article . . ."

Here it comes. She sat down on the side of the
bed. "What about it?"

"Well, I was talking to our new publisher last
night at dinner and he definitely wants to make
some changes to our look. Make *California Business* more attractive on the newsstands. You know
the kind of thing."

She grimaced. Unfortunately, she did know.
That memo Wally had shoved at her made the
situation perfectly clear. With even more wariness than before, she asked, "And what does this
have to do with me?"

"I want you to change the focus of your interview with Jesse, uh, Jason Whatshisname. Be a
bit more, uh, *outgoing* with this interview. Get
inside the man's skin. Make him real. Make him
human."

*Make the interview everything Jason asked me
not to write.*

"Is that all?" she asked. Surely Wally the Weasel had something else up his sleeve.

"Not exactly. We need some pictures of him. *Good* pictures. I'm putting a photographer on standby for you. See if you can get him to agree to a photo shoot, maybe sometime midweek?"

"A photo shoot?" Sure. Jason, with his fetish for privacy, was as likely to agree to a session with a photographer as she was to reconcile with her parents! "I'll see what I can do," she said slowly, "but Jason Cooper isn't likely to agree to that."

The Weasel's voice whined on in her ear. "But we need those pix, Ceej! After all, he *is* California's sexiest businessman. We've gotta show the readers why women drool all over him—you *are* drooling, aren't you?"

"Sure, Wally. Drooling." Which wasn't far off the mark, actually, though she'd die before she admitted it to the Weasel. "So you want me to . . ."

"Add some spice. What's he like to do with his lady friends? What's he look like in his skivvies—you think you could get a snap of him in his skivvies? You know." The Weasel's voice dropped to a lecherous whisper. "*Sex.* Sex sells everything these days—including *California Business.*"

"And if he objects?" C.J. asked slowly.

Dead silence, followed by Wally's voice laced

with steel. "Do it anyway. Do it the way I've asked you to, or . . ."

"Or what?"

"Just do it, Ceej." He hung up the phone.

"Jerk," C.J. muttered as she clicked the off button and returned the stare of her reflection in the mirror over the dresser. Tabloid trash. Her boss demanded sleazy tabloid trash. Yet she'd promised Jason. Well, all she'd *actually* promised was to show him the article before it was published and to make sure all the facts were correct. She hadn't said she'd change it to suit him. She hadn't promised him anything really about the tone or nature of the article.

There was another point too. The Weasel had implicitly threatened her job if she refused to do what he wanted. Of course, she planned to quit anyway, once that job offer from *International Living* came through. But, she didn't have anything official from them yet, just a verbal promise that was worth nothing more than the paper it wasn't written on. She'd kicked around the business world enough to know that counting job offers before receiving them on paper was like counting the proverbial chickens. She might have every reason to expect a formal job offer, but until she held the written proof in her hand, she was still working for *California Business*.

Besides, she might as well get used to writing the kind of article the Weasel wanted. Once she moved to the high-profile, high-glamour world of *International Living*, that was all she'd be writing. The magazine was long on candid photos of celebrities in compromising situations, and short on Pulitzer Prize–quality investigative articles. If she wanted hard-hitting probes of world-shattering news, *IL* was definitely the wrong place to be.

So. It all added up to doing things her boss's way.

Okay. I can do this. Mentally, she reviewed her list of to-do items one more time. *I just have to be cool. Calm. Professional. In control at all times.* Taking a deep breath, she stood.

Collecting her laptop and other paraphernalia, she abandoned her bedroom and headed downstairs, ready for anything. At least she thought she was prepared, until she rounded a corner of the patio and found herself looking at Jason. In the flesh. Clad in a pair of ratty denim shorts and a T-shirt, he defined the word *hunk*. She faltered to a stop, suddenly realizing that her final review of that mental to-do list contained one item she hadn't checked off.

She hadn't actually promised herself not to kiss Jason Cooper again.

But she had little time to re-form her defenses. "Good morning." Excellent . . . cool, professional, in control. Just the right approach.

Crouched, Jason looked up from washing the wheel covers of his metallic-green Ford Explorer. For the first time, she realized it was covered with ash and dust from the fire. In the excitement last night, she hadn't noticed the grime.

"Hi," he said. "Hope I didn't wake you."

She shook her head, glad it didn't audibly rattle. "Um, do you mind if I make some coffee?"

He grimaced and tossed the sponge into the bucket beside him. "Some host, huh? My mom would have my head for not offering breakfast." Straightening, he arched his back. "Let me fix you something to eat."

C.J. trailed him through the patio doors and into the family room. She perched on one of the stools at the breakfast bar while he washed his hands at the kitchen sink. "I'm sorry for interrupting you. You don't really have to cook anything for me." She sounded exactly the way she wanted, as if that kiss last night hadn't affected her at all.

"Don't worry. I won't." He pulled out a package of blueberry muffins, heated one in the microwave, and served it with a mug of coffee.

While she munched in silence and kept a wary eye on Sam, who gobbled his can of cat food with unrestrained greed, she studied Jason's face. He leaned against the counter sipping a glass of orange juice. Slight lines beside his eyes and mouth—lines she didn't recall from yesterday—sparked her reporter's instincts. And when added to the tense way he held his head and shoulders . . .

"Is everything all right?" she asked.

His eyes met hers briefly, then looked away. "Sure."

"I guess I interrupted you washing your car." She took another bite, then put the muffin down.

"It'll keep."

Damn. Back to the terse answers that were the bane of any interviewer. It was like starting all over again. Do not pass Go, do not collect two hundred dollars. She kept her eyes on her mug of coffee while she tried to understand his point of view. Did he resent her intrusion on his privacy? It had been his idea that she stay in the guest room last night. Maybe the best tactic would be to get out of his face. Never mind what the Weasel wanted, she had to make this interview work, and a reluctant, uncooperative subject wouldn't do.

"Do you have a phone book I can borrow?"

"Sure," he said, "over on the bookshelves. Why?"

She pushed away her coffee and swiveled toward the shelves. "I need to call some hotels and try to get a room for tonight."

"You can stay here." The words erupted from him, and she turned to stare. His eyes had widened as if he were as astonished as she at his abrupt statement. Not to mention that his tone wouldn't have won any points from the Martha Stewart School of Gracious Invitations. Still, he *had* officially invited her, and the set of his jaw indicated that he didn't intend to rescind the invitation—no matter how much he might regret having made it in the first place.

"Are you sure? I don't want to impose."

"No problem." The words gritted out. "There's plenty of room."

He obviously was ambivalent about whatever impulse had made him extend the invitation, yet the Weasel wouldn't hesitate to insist she take him up on it. *What does he look like in his skivvies?* Wally's absurd request echoed, and she swallowed hard to try to control the heat rising in her neck. If she stayed, she might actually find out, might actually see—

She smothered that thought by blurting out, "Thanks. I do appreciate it."

The muscles of his jaw relaxed slightly and he nodded once again. Definitely a man of few words. But why had he invited her? This man had more layers than a California freeway had lanes—and each of them ran in a different direction. She smiled for the first time that day. She loved doing profiles of fascinating people, and Jason Cooper was turning into the most intriguing person she'd ever met.

"Well, if that's settled, what's on the agenda for the day?" she asked brightly.

He shrugged and sipped his juice. "Usual stuff. Wash the car. Run some errands. Do some chores. Boring, really."

What happened to the guy who'd kissed her silly last night? Who'd really talked to her about her life and his? And how could she get him to come back? Ignoring the frisson of anticipation that shivered down her spine at that notion, she groped for a way to infiltrate Jason's barriers.

"Do you want some help with the car?"

He inspected her silk blouse with a quizzical lift of his brow. "Dressed like that? I don't think so."

"I can change clothes."

"Why would you want to?"

Hoping his question meant he really wanted an answer, she said, "It's a good way to get to know you. By participating in what you're doing, I can get a better sense of what your life is truly like." All her calm control came at a price, she noticed as she deliberately loosened her grip on the mug's handle. Her knuckles ached with her relaxed grip.

"Hmm. Washing the car. Not exactly profound, is it?"

She shrugged, trying to be just as offhand. "It's a start."

Decisively, he carried his empty glass to the sink, rinsed it, and put it in the dishwasher. "I'll be outside."

Before C.J. could take a breath, he disappeared out the patio doors. Only then did she realize that Jason's one-word answers served the same purpose as her ultraprofessional clothes and in-control demeanor.

They were both in full armor. And if she

wanted to get under his shield, she would have to lower her own.

If she could find the courage to do so.

An hour later Jason's mental vow to keep C.J. at arm's length was unraveling around the edges. As soon as he'd walked back out of the house, he'd berated himself for utter stupidity. What had possessed him to invite the enemy into his own home? He wanted to get rid of her, right? He wanted her to leave him alone, right? And he'd just had a hellish night because he couldn't stop thinking about her sleeping just down the hall, right?

So why the hell had he set himself up for more of the same?

Then, only a few minutes after he returned to washing the car, she'd reappeared, having shed her intimidating power persona for a pair of tight-fitting cutoffs and a comfortably loose T-shirt. She's not a bit sexy, Jason silently assured himself. No way was she irresistible. Not even close. He could handle her unwanted presence just fine. Of course he could.

Until, that is, with miles-long legs and a determined glint in her eyes, C.J. plunged into the car washing and waxing with enthusiasm and an almost childish glee.

He handed her the hose, being careful not to

brush her fingers with his. "Here. You do the top while I finish the wheel covers."

What a mistake. His crouching position as he scrubbed the wheel covers and applied a rubber protector to the tires left him eyeball-to-kneecap intimate with the most tempting legs he'd encountered in many a day. She stretched on tiptoes to reach the car's roof while his body did its own stretching—to the front of his jeans.

Irritated, he switched wheels to move away from those legs.

When he found himself across the car's hood from her while she polished the surface, he started to relax . . . only to tense again as he watched her rhythmic motions. Hell. It wasn't as if she were deliberately tempting him. He didn't even think she was aware that he was watching her work. Her movements were neat, precise, controlled, not seductive and coy. But something about the way she muscled polish onto the hood's glossy surface made him wonder if she'd apply that same determined enthusiasm to love-making.

He decided some conversation might lift his mind above his belt buckle.

"Thanks for your help with this. I usually do it myself." Clever start. Mentally, he whapped his forehead in disgust.

"You're welcome. Actually"—a glance revealed her impish grin—"I'm kind of enjoying it. It's been a long time since I polished a car."

"You don't own a car?" Didn't *everyone* have a car in California? It was practically a necessity when getting to the grocery store might be a several-mile trek and efficient public transportation was more wishful thinking than reality.

"Oh, sure. Gertrude runs like a champ. I just don't polish her."

Appalled, he sat back on his heels. "How could you neglect a fine piece of machinery like that? Good maintenance is the key to keeping a car running perfectly."

She wiped a strand of hair out of her eye with the back of a dirty hand. "Oh, I maintain her—oil changes and stuff like that. I just don't bother too much with how she looks."

"But—but—" He hardly knew how to respond to such blasphemy.

She laughed. "Sputtered like a guy who works with cars for a living. Tell me, do you tuck this baby in bed every night?"

"Certainly not," he said stiffly. "I keep it garaged to protect it from the sun and wind, but—"

"I knew it!" She laughed with the delight of someone who'd opened an oyster and discovered a pearl.

For some reason, her humor was infectious and he found his mouth curling upward. "Are you laughing at me?"

"Of course not." She tried to choke off her snickers.

He frowned briefly, but gave it up. "Well, don't stifle yourself on my account."

After that, the work went faster. Curiosity, still lurking from last night, finally unglued his tongue and he asked, "Where do you live, anyway?"

"In the Bay Area. I've got a small apartment in Sausalito."

"Ah. Artsy-craftsy, huh?"

"Not exactly. I just lucked into a place that's actually affordable. Most of the neighborhood is way out of my price range."

"Do you like living there?"

"It's all right." She shrugged. "I'll be leaving soon anyway."

He gave her a quick glance and saw her grimace. Her expression reminded him of Sam's after the cat had just purloined one of Jason's favorite popcorn-flavored Jelly Bellies from the bowl on the kitchen counter. Jason wouldn't mind so much if Sam ate the candies, but the cat merely liked to play kitty soccer with them because they made a satisfying rattle and scooted easily across the floor. Jason was forever finding them in odd corners, usually right after his foot smushed them into the flooring. C.J.'s face displayed that same combination of guilt, regret, and sheer pleasure that Sam's did when confronted with the results of his sins.

Tossing his sponge down, Jason stood and

stretched while trying to make his question seem casual. "You're moving somewhere else?"

She propped her fists on her hips and glared at him. "Damn! What is it with you? Every time I'm around you I turn into a motormouth."

He spread his hands in a disclaimer and tried to look like he hadn't deliberately pried into her private life. "Hey, I'm a trustworthy kind of guy. People tell me all their secrets."

"I don't."

He grinned. "I think you just did." Not allowing time for her chagrin to freeze her tongue, he rushed on. "Where are you planning to move to?"

"I suppose it doesn't matter much if you know," she muttered before returning to her polishing. "I'm waiting for the paperwork on a new job offer to reach me. When it does, I'm resigning from *California Business* to work for *International Living* magazine. I'll be a roving reporter, sent all over the world to report on how the other half lives."

"Sounds like fun," Jason said, deliberately keeping his voice neutral.

"Yeah, it will be. I've worked hard for a long time to get this offer."

To Jason, her voice conveyed all the longing of a wild bird penned in a cage. "So you'll be doing a lot of traveling?"

She grinned. "I don't have that passport I

showed you last night for nothing. I'm going to fill it up with stamps from all over the world."

"I see." He let that sink in and pretended his stomach hadn't knotted. "Aren't you going to miss your friends? Family?"

"Not me. I don't have any ties. I'm free as a bird."

An old song teased his memory, something about freedom and not having anything left to lose. Was that the case with C.J.? Had she already lost everything that mattered?

His jaw clenched shut to keep the questions from boiling out. Where she went or what she did after she finished her profile of him was none of his business. Determined to throttle his unruly thoughts into submission, he grabbed another rag and started buffing the dried polish. The only concession he gave to the swirling in his gut was to make sure to keep the width of the car between him and C.J.

Industriously, he rubbed harder while he tried to convince himself he didn't care that soon she'd fly out of his reach forever.

When the Explorer gleamed in pristine splendor under a cloudless sky, Jason watched C.J. collapse onto the low stone wall with a boneless grace that put Sam to shame.

"We did good," she announced with an impish grin. "That sucker couldn't be more gorgeouser."

Jason handed her a frosty glass of iced tea and sprawled into a patio chair. "Yeah. Thanks for your help." He took a long swallow, then set his glass aside.

Between them, they'd polished, waxed, and shined the vehicle into better-than-showroom glory. "You know, it's so shiny, it almost hurts to look at it," C.J. commented.

"You worked hard." He shifted uncomfortably, then added, "I really hadn't meant to do a complete detail job on it this morning, you know."

"But with a willing slave to help, you couldn't resist?"

"Something like that, I guess."

"That's me, slave to the sexiest businessman in California." Her salaam was a pretty decent one, given that she made no attempt to move off the stone wall.

"Have a lot of experience as a slave, do you?"

"None at all. That's why I'm so good at it."

He grinned at her sassiness, but didn't respond. His gut tightened yet again with the now familiar urge to grab her and hold her tight. *Damn.* Wouldn't you know the first woman who seriously interested him in months would be one who planned to flee the country faster than he could change a tire.

Cautiously, he let his gaze rest on her. She

straddled the two-foot-high wall and leaned back on her elbows, letting the warmth of the sun cascade over her cheeks and neck. With the relaxed sensuality of a cat she slowly dragged the dewy glass over her face to cool herself, a move that parched Jason's throat to Sahara aridity. Sunlight illuminated gold highlights in her hair, luring him to run his fingers through it. Was it as soft as he remembered from last night? Did it still smell of cinnamon and wildflowers?

He shut his eyes, but couldn't completely tune out her voice, softly humming a lively tune. Nor could he keep his belly from clenching every time a hint of spice and roses drifted his way.

Why was he doing this to himself? She'd already admitted that she had one foot out the door and the other ready to follow. Why get involved with a woman who wouldn't be around long enough to matter? Besides, he barely knew her. How could he *know* that she was the one for him when they'd only met the day before?

Jason excelled at facing facts. He prided himself on his realistic assessment of situations and events; it was one of the reasons he was an excellent business manager. But as he sat in the morning sunshine and studiously avoided looking at C.J., only one fact held any importance. He wanted her. And just as he'd always trusted his logic, he also trusted his instincts. Right now they all screamed at him to tie C.J. to him with every irrevocable bond he could possibly construct.

He had to find a way to keep her around long enough to discover if she truly was the woman for him. And then he had to figure out how to keep her with him—permanently.

Or else, he feared, his heart might never recover.

SIX

"Baby-sitting? You're going to baby-sit a set of triplets on a Saturday night?" C.J.'s voice held a definite squeak.

Jason pretended to consider his answer carefully. "No, I don't think that's quite accurate."

"Oh. Good. I knew I must have misunderstood—"

"The more accurate statement is *we're* going to baby-sit a set of triplets tonight." He arched a quizzical eyebrow. "You did say you were going to be my shadow for this week, didn't you?"

She dithered beautifully, he had to admit, while he tucked her into his Explorer. He was more interested in watching her than in paying attention to her protests. They wouldn't change anything anyway. He'd promised Rome to look after the kids and that meant she was going along too. Mentally he rubbed his hands in satisfaction.

This was going to work out perfectly. He flicked on the ignition and headed for Rome's house.

The day had gone surprisingly well, all things considered. Wise enough to learn from his experience while washing the car, he made a point of keeping far enough away from C.J. to control his impulses—though it wasn't easy. There was something naturally tempting about her, though he'd be willing to bet Rome's season tickets to the Chargers that she had no idea how much she lured him. On the surface, she was all business, but underneath . . .

What was underneath? Was she really a focused, career-driven businesswoman who scorned all family ties? Or was that merely a disguise meant to protect a softer, more vulnerable C.J.?

He vowed that tonight he'd find out.

He had the perfect plan in mind too. This was going to be a snap. His triplet nieces were, bar none, the cutest pixies on the planet— naturally, a strictly unbiased opinion. If C.J. had a heart at all, it would melt when she saw Samantha, Sydney, and Alexandra at their most adorable. If they didn't convince even the family-hating C.J. that ties didn't necessarily have to bind uncomfortably, he'd . . . he'd eat the grungiest pair of sweatsocks he owned!

It was going to be hell munching on sweat-socks tartare.

After three hours of baby-sitting, Jason was ready to throw in the towel. C.J. had no heart. How else to explain her complete resistance to all things adorable in his nieces?

Case in point. By the time they'd been at Rome's house half an hour, he'd already begun silently congratulating himself on his brilliant strategy. As usual, the three-and-a-half-year-old triplets had wrapped their Unca Jase around their collective fingers. And if they could do that to a macho guy like him, what hope did the feminine C.J. have to keep herself aloof? That bet with himself was going to be a slam dunk.

Sydney, the leader of the pack and the oldest by a mere seven minutes, had convinced him to play an unintelligible game of cards on the floor. Gentle Samantha, the peacemaker of the three, was also playing cards, while independent Alexandra had conned C.J. into inspecting her entire collection of dolls.

"Are you sure you understand the rules of that game?" C.J.'s amused question distracted him, allowing Syd to snatch another two cards from his hand. C.J. sat on the sofa behind him, with Alex at her side nattering in a soft monotone a story about one of her dolls.

"No," he admitted. "But Syd here knows them. And she wouldn't let me make a mistake. Would you, Syd?"

Limpid blue-green eyes the exact shade of Rome's stared up at him with perfect innocence. "No, Unca Jase." Her caramel curls bounced as she shook her head earnestly.

"See?" He made the mistake of turning to wink at C.J.

"*My* turn now! Unca Jase, watch me play!" Sydney retrieved his attention. Those limpid eyes now shot sparks of irritation.

"But you just played your hand, Syd. Doesn't Samantha get a turn now?"

"No! My turn!"

Samantha's chin quivered, but she nodded. " 'S okay."

"No, Sydney, that's not fair." Jason put his hand firmly over Sydney's to stop the little girl from snatching more cards. "You have to play by the rules. It's Samantha's turn now."

"But I wanna play now. Why can't I play now, Unca Jase?" Outrageously long lashes batted at him in practiced flirtation.

Ignoring a choked cough from C.J., he said, "Because you told me the rule was that we'd all take turns. Isn't that the way we play? And it's Sam's turn." He gave Sam an encouraging smile. "Go ahead, honey, and play your cards."

Obviously uncertain, Samantha tentatively took a card from Sydney's hand. While her sister glowered Sam triumphantly laid down a trio of kitten-pictured cards. "Kitties, Unca Jase! I got the kitties. They're my fav'rite."

"Good for you, Sam—"

Jason's congratulations were interrupted by Sydney's sudden explosion. "Don't like this game!" With the sweep of her hand, she pushed all the cards into a messy pile. Before he quite knew how it happened, Sam was in tears and Syd had erupted into howls of frustration. Meanwhile, Alex ignored the uproar and kept up a continual stream of chatter.

When he finally calmed his two little ladies down and dared a glance at C.J., he saw her purse her lips in a frown as disapproving as the union rep's at the start of the company's last contract negotiations.

Evidently, Sydney's creative cardplaying strategy hadn't melted C.J.'s heart even the tiniest bit.

Unfortunately, the evening went downhill from there. Jason soon realized exactly why his sister had insisted on an evening away from her brood. The girls' moods quickly segued from adorably fractious to downright whiny. Samantha clung to his legs so tightly that he could barely move, Sydney's flirty jealousy only exacerbated her sister's clinging, and Alexandra chattered so constantly that her voice became hoarse.

Not to mention that none of them could keep from whining for something—a drink, a game, a story, whatever—for more than three and a half minutes at a time. And usually all at the same time.

By bedtime even Jason could see that the kids' behavior wasn't just the usual childish irritation. All three showed the overbright eyes and flushed cheeks of a fever. And though C.J. helped him put the little girls to bed with no overt comment, he had a sinking feeling that Sydney's biting C.J.'s hand and Alexandra's vomiting all over C.J.'s black tailored slacks hadn't helped his cause a bit.

He called Rome and Lyssa on their cell phone, and within half an hour the anxious parents had returned, relieving Jason and C.J. of their charges. Good thing, too, he thought darkly as he ushered C.J. out the door. Any more of his nieces' "adorableness" and she'd likely add "family" and "children" to her list of unspeakably profane concepts.

God, those kids were charmers! C.J. settled gratefully into the leather seat of Jason's Explorer. It had taken all her self-control not to hug each one of the little girls and rock them to sleep. She'd forgotten—had deliberately chosen not to remember—how utterly winsome little kids could be.

But they're not for you. You're never going to tie yourself down with a family, remember?

Yeah, she remembered. At moments like this she wished she didn't.

Think of all the ways kids tie you down. Schools. Sitters. Pediatrician visits. Dentist appointments. What a pain.

And let's not forget hugs, cuddles, and chocolate-milk kisses, she mentally retorted before she could stop herself. She forced the twinge of longing back into a shadowed corner of her mind. None of that mattered. She wasn't meant to have a family, and that was that.

Beside her, Jason hesitated before taking his hand off the ignition. He shifted in the driver's seat to half face her. "Sorry about all that." A gesture toward the house encompassed the less-than-successful evening. "I didn't know the kids were sick."

She shrugged, trying to sound nonchalant. "That's all right. It's one of those things. You don't suppose they're seriously ill, do you?" *Darn it.* She hadn't meant to let her concern escape.

"Nah. Lyssa said several of the kids in their play group recently had similar symptoms. It's probably one of those twenty-four-hour bugs that kids get." Even in the dim light from the dash, she caught his questioning glance. "You sound worried about them."

She let that slide by without response. "You're very good with your nieces."

"Yep. They've got their Uncle Jase wrapped around their little fingers, all right."

"I could tell." More sure of her control, she risked meeting his gaze.

Silence stretched between them like the first tentative silken strand of a web-building spider. Finally, Jason looked away. "It's only eight-thirty. Why don't we get something to eat? I don't know about you, but those kids make me hungry."

"We ate earlier, remember?"

A wry grin kicked up the corners of his mouth. "And your point is . . . ?"

Alarm bells clanged in C.J.'s head as she recognized how tempting that invitation was. Jason had asked her as if she were a date, a desired companion for the evening. And while the inclination to accept and simply enjoy the experience was as tempting as chocolate toffee ripple ice cream, she couldn't afford to let herself relax that much.

She had to convince herself—and Jason—that any personal relationship between them simply wouldn't work. He was her profile subject, not a date. More than that, he was hearth and home and family, and she was . . .

Well, she just wasn't.

She forced her lips into a polite but cool smile. "That would be very nice, thank you, Jason. And perhaps we could continue the interview over dinner?"

His gaze lasered into hers. "I take it you

wouldn't be accepting if it weren't for the interview?"

She hardened herself to speak logically. "I wouldn't be here at all if it weren't for that."

"I see." His fingers drummed against the steering wheel. "You're right," he said finally. "So why don't we just go home and forget about eating."

It wasn't a question. Before she could reply, he'd started the car and headed toward his house. In the few minutes it took to arrive, she mentally chastised herself. *See what your all-work-and-no-play insistence did? You blew your chance to be with him!*

Yes, but I'll be alone with him at his house, she thought. It's a lot more intimate there. We'll have plenty of privacy to—

To what? Delve deeper into his psyche? Learn about his childhood dreams? Discover his most profound thoughts? Or . . .

All that, she retorted silently. And what "or" do you mean? She couldn't disguise her defensive edge from herself.

Or find out if he looks half as good in his boxers as you've imagined he does. Even confirm if he wears boxers or briefs. Darn, but her mental self was developing a sarcastic tone. A shiver skittered along her nerves at the images that heated her imagination. All she really wanted, she assured herself, was the chance to continue the interview.

"Are you coming in?" Jason's question interrupted her mental debate.

"What? Sure." Hastily she gathered her purse and followed him into the house.

Jason immediately headed for the kitchen, grabbing his cordless phone along the way. While he rummaged in the refrigerator she saw him punching buttons, apparently to retrieve his phone messages.

She was considering what question to ask first when he stiffened and stood upright, his gaze fixed on her and an unfathomable expression clouding his face.

"Well, that's it," he said when he'd pressed a couple more buttons to clear his messages.

"What's 'it'?"

"We can't do any more talking tonight. I've got to hit the sack early."

"But it's not even nine o'clock!"

He shrugged, pouring a large glass of milk. His gestured want-some? query bounced off her. "Doesn't matter. I've gotta be up very early tomorrow—by six."

"On a Sunday morning?"

"Yes. But you don't have to tag along. We'll pick things up sometime later—maybe Monday morning."

"All right, Cooper," she said, her fists propped on her hips. "What's going on?"

He pulled out a bakery sack of chocolate

thumbprint cookies and munched one before answering. "It's simple. Our company OTL team lost someone to injury today. We're in contention for a trophy, so I'm filling in tomorrow. Which means I have to go to early church, which means I have to get up at six. Simple."

But C.J. was lost back at the beginning of his explanation. "OTL? What's OTL?"

"The Over the Line tournament ends this weekend. It's a little like softball—sort of. It's played down on Fiesta Island. Tomorrow are the finals."

She eyed him closely. He was being deliberately obstructive, she was sure. "How come I've never heard of Over the Line?"

His mouth twitched in what looked suspiciously like a suppressed grin. "It's a San Diego tradition. It's not played very many other places. But it's kind of a guy thing. Why don't you take the day off and I'll meet with you again on Monday? Have you been to the San Diego Zoo yet? You might catch a good view of the new panda habitat. Want me to call and find out what times they'll be on display tomorrow?"

He was up to something, but what? For some reason he didn't want her to go to this sporting event. She didn't know why, but every one of her instincts was screaming at her, insisting that the one place she really *had* to go tomorrow was down to Fiesta Island to see this Over the Line tournament for herself.

So she smiled and said demurely, "Pandas, hmmm? That would be fine. Do you think there's someplace I can rent a car for the day?"

His relief was so patent she had to smother her own grin. "No problem. In fact, I've got a car I can lend you. It's nothing fancy, but . . ."

She didn't even get a chance to thank him before he'd punched in some numbers on the phone, listened intently, and scribbled some notes on a scrap of paper.

"Here are the times the pandas will be on public view. If you're there at nine, you should get in before the crowds get too bad. I'm a member of the Zoological Society. Do you want a free guest pass?"

My, my, my. Isn't he being helpful? He must really want you someplace else. Agreeably she took the free pass he dug out of a drawer and handed her along with the slip of paper with panda viewing times scribbled on it. Just as agreeably, she yawned, and headed upstairs to the guest room for the night. She had work to do.

Half an hour later, having used her computer to tap into the on-line archives of the *San Diego Union-Tribune*, her eyes widened. So he was going to play in the Over the Line tournament, was he? So it was a "guy thing," was it? An understatement if she'd ever heard one.

A pertinent reference sent her to the Web site of the tournament's sponsor, the Old Mission Beach Athletic Club—OMBAC for short. There she found the rules for OTL, as well as details of a fascinating contest to name some buxom beauty "Ms. Emerson," and photos of the action at the previous year's tournament. OMBAC's annual OTL tournament was quite an occasion, it seemed. She snickered softly when she read the alternate translation of OMBAC as "Old Men Behaving as Children."

Staring at the pictures and info she'd downloaded, she became more determined than ever to follow Jason to Fiesta Island.

San Diego's Over the Line tournament: Two full weekends devoted to sand, sun, surf . . . and salaciousness. Oh, yeah. And some people— a few—actually played the mysterious game called Over the Line.

She could hardly wait to see if Jason's Mr. Clean image could survive the hijinks.

Jason sprawled on his bed. He'd sure as hell squeaked through that one! Tomorrow morning after church he'd send C.J. off to look at the animals in the zoo, relieved that she wasn't going to be anywhere close to Fiesta Island—where the *real* animals hung out.

It was one of those good news/bad news situations. On the one hand, he'd love to get her in a situation where she could let her hair down a bit—and the OTL tournament certainly involved undoing a lot of hair. Not to mention bikini tops. On the other, he had a very primitive reaction to the thought of her parading her charms in front of a bunch of leering guys who were, well, animals.

So it was best that she was going to stay away from the games. He'd just have to imagine her standing on the sidelines, cheering him on. He could see it now. She'd be wearing one of those teeny string bikinis and she'd clap madly every time he scored a hit. Which would be every at-bat, of course, since he really was a pretty damned good player. And, after the Golden Auto Parts team won their division, she'd throw herself into his arms, congratulate him with a big kiss, and . . .

His fantasies holding sway, he drifted to sleep, a sensual smile curving his mouth.

By the time she hiked from the shuttle-bus drop-off point to the OTL playing grounds on the beach, C.J. had been propositioned four times. A wry downward glance at herself left her shaking her head in wonder. She was no beach bunny, though she had dressed appropriately in cutoffs and a halter. She had a bottle of sun-screen tucked into her bag, dark glasses perched on her nose, and a floppy hat on her head.

No doubt this tournament was the perfect place for her to find out what Jason was really like when he wasn't pretending to be Mr. Squeaky Clean. She'd been building him up in her mind as the ideal man, and that had to stop. No man was perfect, not even Jason, and once she'd proved that little fact to herself, her silly heart could stop ka-thumping every time she was within sight of him.

She hoped.

But in the meantime, what about her was so attractive to all these guys with hyperactive gonads?

"Don't worry about it. It's all in fun. They don't mean anything by it."

The voice materializing beside her made C.J. spin around to face a bikini-clad beauty wearing a friendly smile.

"What?" C.J. asked. God, she could feel herself sprouting wrinkles just looking at the other girl's perfect body and youthful face. Not to mention the prominent breasts all but bursting from the minuscule bikini top.

"I said, don't worry about the propositions. It's just part of the game at OTL." The girl tipped her head in inquiry. "This your first tournament?"

"Yes. I'm from out of town and decided to stop by because . . ." How could she explain her reasons to this girl?

But she didn't seem to notice C.J.'s hesitation. "Well, then, welcome! I'm Darla Martinez. Ms. Emerson first runner-up."

C.J. shook Darla's extended hand. "I'm C. J. Stone. I'm a writer for *California Business.*"

"A writer! That's great! You here to do a feature on the tournament?"

"Not exactly. I'm profiling one of the players. He's on the team from Golden Auto Parts."

"You mean the 'Golden, Schmolden, Let's Just Do It' team? They're in contention for the title in the Men's Century Division." From a teensy purse draped over her shoulder and hanging against her hip, Darla produced a much-folded program schedule. "Let's see. They're playing over on court three starting at, um, eleven. I'll take you there if you like."

"Sure, thanks." C.J. fell into step beside the buxom brunette.

"So which player are you profiling?" Darla asked. "Some of them are really cute. Old, maybe, but cute." She giggled in a way that made C.J. feel like she'd just added another decade.

"Jason Cooper. He's substituting for someone who was hurt yesterday."

Darla stopped dead. "The Coop? The Coop's playing this year after all?"

"If you mean Jason Cooper, then, yes. At least he's playing today anyway." C.J. eyed the girl. "You know him?"

"Oooh, yeah!" She giggled again. "He's a real hunk . . . you know what I mean? I didn't think I'd get to see him here this year. He's been my favorite for, like *years*. Him and me, we're like *that*." She held up two fingers intertwined, accompanied by another giggle and a coy blush.

C.J. double-checked her estimate of Darla's age. If the girl had passed her eighteenth birthday, it was a miracle of rapid maturation. So how could Jason have been involved with her for "years"?

Grimly, she steered Darla toward the spectator area surrounding court three. "Let's find a place where we can watch the game. And would you mind if I asked you some questions about Jason?"

Darla's eyes opened wide. "You mean like an *interview*? You want to interview *me*? Wow. This is like, way *cool*!"

C.J. hoped the girl didn't notice her rolling her eyes.

Several hours later confusion fogged C.J.'s mind. Darla had actually *gushed* over Jason, whom she'd known since she was eight or nine. But despite all of C.J.'s careful probes, she learned precisely nothing about Jason or his relationship to the buxom Darla.

The thing was, C.J. hardly knew whether to be relieved or sorry.

C.J. stayed carefully out of his sight throughout the afternoon, but managed to keep him under close observation. As best she could tell, he hadn't noticed her presence, hovering in the background of the thousands of revelers. Of course, it was no hardship to spend her time staring at the muscles rippling under his tanned back and chest. Or to imagine his strong legs rubbing against her own. By the time his first five-inning game ended with a win, she had to find a cold drink vendor and cool herself off.

He played the mysterious, incomprehensible game well, as judged by the roars of approval whenever he caught the ball or hit it successfully. But win or lose, he was, in her eyes, the most dynamically attractive man there.

As the afternoon sunshine started to dim and the first wisps of the early-evening fog and low clouds drifted in, Jason's team was playing for the Century Division championship. C.J. found herself caught up in the excitement of the game. She'd picked up enough of the rules through the afternoon to have some notion of what was going on, though she found it hard to tear her gaze from Jason to watch other players.

With the score tied at the end of the fifth inning, the game went into extra innings. The other team batted first in the sixth and scored three runs—an enormous lead, given the skill of the players involved.

C.J. edged closer to the front of the crowd to watch as Jason's three-man team came to bat. After two outs, the three mythical bases were "loaded," and Jason moved into batting position. One of his teammates knelt beside him and pitched the ball, while C.J. held her breath in anticipation. Could Jason get another hit? Two foul balls would get that third out and the game would be over.

But with a sharp crack of the bat, the ball soared over the head of the opposing fielders, staying centered between the two foul lines. Jason had cleared the bases with a home run, scoring four runs and winning the game!

C.J. jumped up and down and screamed ecstatically. The press of the crowd pushed her forward onto the playing court to congratulate the new champions and celebrate their victory. As she was shoved ever closer she saw Jason's eyes widen as, for the first time that day, he noticed her in the crowd.

"Congratulations!" her lips formed, though she knew he'd never be able to hear her in the bedlam.

His eyes locked on hers and he started to move toward her, a question lighting his gaze with a sensual promise that fizzed through C.J.'s veins. Her feet cemented to the soft sand, she didn't breathe for fear that this moment would be lost.

"Jason! You did it!" Darla elbowed her way through the crowd to grab Jason's arm and hug it to her. On his other side, another beach beauty clad in a bikini even scanter than Darla's grabbed his arm, pulled his head down, and plastered a huge kiss right on his mouth.

The kiss shook C.J. back to her senses. She wasn't here to respond to Jason's incredible masculinity! She was here to learn more about him— and the more sensational the news the better. What could be more revealing than him standing there, clad only in cutoffs, and with each arm filled by a nearly naked beach bunny? Even the smear of bloodred lipstick across his mouth added to the overall image of a man who would fit right in at the Playboy Mansion.

Slowly, she raised her camera to eye level, intending to capture at least this one image for her article. Through the viewfinder, she saw yet another string-bikini-clad babe sashay up to Jason, put her arms around his neck, and lower his head to hers. A ribbon draped around her declared her MS. EMERSON 1997—a title that she'd learned was a cleaned-up version of a guy's crude " 'em are *some* . . ." assessment of women's breasts.

The picture wouldn't get any sexier than this. Three babes and a beach-bum hero. She focused through the viewfinder as Ms. Emerson's lips locked onto Jason's. Her finger found the shutter just as he looked straight at the camera, his face showing disapproval, disappointment, and something else she couldn't quite define. . . .

She couldn't press the button.

She lowered the camera and turned away. She'd failed. She couldn't—wouldn't—take such a photo, not of Jason. How could she?

She loved him.

SEVEN

Jason shook off his bevy of beauties and took three long strides to where C.J. stood frozen, her camera held at waist level. His heart thudded with the exhilaration of winning the game, the excitement of the crowd's congratulations, the exhaustion of playing hard all afternoon . . .

. . . and the sheer intoxication of realizing that his fantasies from last night had come true. C.J. was here, cheering him to victory.

Well, okay, not *all* his fantasies had come true. For one thing, her sensible shorts and halter covered far too much of her, compared with his erotic imaginings of last night. On the other hand, it was better by far that the unclaimed beach bunnies showed off their assets than that C.J. did. She was taken.

Taken?

Jolted by his instinctive desire to grab and

hold, he settled for his hands on her shoulders. "I didn't expect to see you here."

"I know." Her head tipped upward, allowing the breeze to waft a strand of silky cinnamon hair to tickle the back of his hand. "That's why I decided to come."

"Remind me not to underestimate your initiative in the future."

The curve of her mouth in a slightly smug smile tempted him more than he wanted to admit. His gaze locked onto her pink lips for two thundering heartbeats before he met her eyes again.

"So, where's my kiss of congratulations?" he asked.

Her fingers traced the edge of his mouth. "You've already had one—two actually. The first from one of your admirers and the other from Ms. Emerson. The lipstick shows—right here."

He wanted a kiss from *her*, not some over-sexed bombshell who was already consoling the losers. "So wipe it off me. Or maybe replace her lipstick with yours."

"I'm not wearing any. Just a sunscreen lip gloss."

Her fingertips still lingered by his mouth, so he knew it wasn't much of a protest. "And your point is . . . ?"

She gave a shaky laugh and admitted, "I haven't the vaguest idea."

"Good." Without giving her a chance to lose

her nerve, he dipped his head and touched his mouth to hers.

His lips savored her gloss-slick flesh, sliding into position to perfectly cover her mouth. He nibbled tentatively, not really wanting to push the kiss too far or too fast, just basking in her warmth. But when her mouth opened slightly, the temptation to send his tongue exploring pushed him over the edge. His tongue dove inside in a hungry, insistent kiss, his hands pulling her hard against him. His mind spun with pleasure. The clamor of the happy crowd around them faded as he concentrated entirely on enjoying the sensations spiraling out of control within him.

Until, that is, someone shoved against C.J.'s back and they tumbled to the sand, with C.J. on top.

"Hey, Coop, none of that here!" A raucous laugh and the chatter of the surrounding watchers finally impinged on his consciousness.

Jason checked C.J. for damage. "You all right?"

"Uh-huh. I landed on top. How about you?"

On top of him was right. In fact, she straddled him. He was torn. He didn't really want her to move, but if she didn't get off him soon . . .

She levered herself off him and stood, then extended a hand to help him up.

"Doesn't look like I did too much damage,"

she commented, brushing him down to remove the sand clinging to his skin.

The patting motions of her hands against his bare back and legs tested his control to the limit. He stepped away from her. "That's okay. I can do it."

"Hey, Jase! You gonna come celebrate with us?" Diego Lopez, one of his OTL teammates, gestured at a small crowd of revelers, including the busty Ms. Emerson.

He quirked an eyebrow at C.J. in silent query. "You want to join them?"

She shrugged, though he fancied he could see a trace of disappointment in her eyes. "It's up to you. I'm here to find out more about what *you* like, remember?"

Why did she have to keep bringing up that stupid article just as he thought he was making progress? He opened his mouth to ask that very question, when the answer practically clunked him on the head.

It's a defense mechanism, stupid. She's using the article to keep from throwing herself at you.

Yeah. That was probably it. His grin was probably as sappy as a seventeen-year-old confronted with his first prom date as he tried to absorb the implications of that insight. "You guys go on without me," he called to his buddies, turning down their invitation. "I've got other things to do."

Ignoring the hoots and catcalls that speculated just what those "other things" might be with C.J. for company, he asked her quietly, "You don't mind, do you? Not partying hard, I mean."

She shrugged, but surely that glint in her eye meant approval. "Whatever you want."

If he told her what he *really* wanted, he'd shock her down to her toenails. Prudently, he said, "Well, Rome and Lyssa are half expecting me for dinner. Would you like to join us?"

She tipped her head sideways. "What is it with you and Rome? Do you always spend so much free time with his family?"

"Nah. It's just the only way I get to see my three nieces. And I have to straighten Rome out occasionally." His voice dropped as if he were confiding a corporate secret. "The man thinks he knows sports. Trust me, he doesn't. I'm gonna collect big on the Padres game tonight."

"Hmm. Another 'guy thing,' right?"

In companionable silence, they made their way back to the shuttle bus pickup point. Jason held C.J.'s hand firmly in his own, unwilling to break that physical link. He felt totally alive, energy sizzling through his veins. They'd won the championship, but more important, he'd seen C.J. back away from that damning photograph. His triumph on the OTL court faded into insignificance compared with the tacit victory C.J. had conceded to him when she'd lowered her camera without pressing the shutter.

He was beginning to win her over, he was sure. A bit more exposure to his nieces and she would see the light about home and family and maybe even understand how love glued families together instead of splitting them apart. And with any luck at all, she might even concede one more victory to him. She just might admit that she and he might be able to make a family of their own.

Together.

Dinner at Rome and Lyssa's house turned out to be an educational experience for C.J. The triplets, apparently having bounced back from their illness of the night before, were lively, charming, and mischievous. They swarmed over their uncle Jason and their father with the total lack of self-consciousness of kids who knew they were truly wanted and loved.

C.J. fought down a surge of envy while she helped Lyssa put the final touches on the meal. In the background the large television showed a baseball game. The team in dark blue shirts was trouncing the team with the gray uniforms. Or maybe it was the other way around.

"Your kids really love Jason," she said quietly to Lyssa. "He's a real family man, isn't he?"

The other woman's intelligent eyes studied C.J.'s face. "You bet. He didn't used to be, of course. When I first told him I wanted to get married, he was against the institution on general bachelor principles. But I ignored him, and once he saw his nieces—wham! That was it. He's been looking for someone to settle down with ever since."

"So he's serious about someone?" An actual pain arrowed through her heart at the thought.

Lyssa smiled and shook her head. "No way. I said he's looking, not that he's found anyone he wants to keep. At least not yet. Though . . ."

C.J. dropped the knife she was using to mangle a basket of cherry tomatoes for the salad. "What is it?"

"Nothing really." Expertly turning the chicken-and-shrimp kabobs on the built-in grill on the stovetop, Lyssa changed the subject. "What about you? Do you want a family?"

"I'm not the home-and-hearth type. I'm more 'good-bye girl' than 'happy homemaker.' " But even C.J. could hear the regret in her words.

Lyssa laughed. "That sounds like what Rome used to say. He was a real traveling man, had all kinds of reasons why he'd never settle down, never get married—or at least not until sometime a long way in the future. But just look at him now."

Rome was comfortably ensconced on the family-room couch, a little girl on each side and a third on his lap, while he tried to explain the intricacies of the infield-fly rule to his toddler audience. As if aware of his wife's scrutiny, he looked up suddenly, and gave Lyssa a smile of such loving sweetness that C.J. felt as if she'd stumbled into a lovers' tryst.

Her gaze skittered away, and latched onto Jason's. The intensity of his look sent a hot tide rushing up her neck and face. Hastily, she broke the contact.

The evening took on a surreal quality as they ate dinner. C.J. was fascinated by the story of Lyssa and Rome's courtship. Perhaps not surprisingly, each had a slightly different take on the dynamics of their relationship during that stormy time.

"It was just a matter of holding out till Rome saw the sweet light of reason," Lyssa explained, with a saucy grin directed at Rome. "Men are a bit slow that way."

"Hmm. As I recall, *you* were the one who needed convincing to marry me." Rome's outrage was blunted by his automatic efforts to help Samantha get her chicken off the skewer.

"Only because you'd worked so hard to convince me—and yourself—that you weren't a good family man."

"Hmmph."

C.J. absorbed everything while saying little herself. An idea was beginning to glimmer in her mind, and she wanted to think it through before she lost it.

"Do you mind if I take a moment or two to

make some notes on my laptop after dinner?" she asked Lyssa later. "I brought it with me."

"Of course not. The dishes are done, the guys are watching the kids and the game. It'll give me a chance to put my feet up for a moment."

"Thanks." C.J. retrieved her computer from the hall and set it up on the dining-room table. It would take only a few minutes to get the gist of her idea down, then she could contemplate how she wanted to develop it.

Talking with Lyssa, her half-formed notion of a book about women in transition suddenly coalesced in her head. The prospect of working on that project she'd envisioned so long ago tempted her mightily. She was filled with sheer joy at the prospect of writing something with genuine meaning and depth. She could see exactly how she'd approach the subject to make it readable yet authoritative. The experts she'd interview. The real-life stories she'd use to keep it human.

Financially, it would be a risk, of course. *But was it any more of a risk than gadding about the world all alone?* Perhaps not, she admitted silently. She had some money tucked away. She could always pick up some freelance work to help tide her over. She could probably swing it okay as far as money went.

Maybe, just maybe, this assignment to interview Jason would be a watershed in her career after all. Not merely because it marked her departure from *California Business*, but also, and more important, because it could mark her own transition from itinerant tabloid hack to serious writer. And if she chose to make that leap of faith in her ability to write a piece with real depth and substance, another reward could be waiting as well.

Jason.

Her realization this afternoon that he'd burrowed his way into her heart still frightened her. She had no idea if she knew how to have a long-term relationship with anyone. Certainly, she'd failed with her own family. And none of her previous relationships had ever progressed much beyond a few weeks. Was she ready to make another try with Jason?

C.J. didn't know. But with her skin crawling with disgust about the trashy article Wally wanted her to write, she was beginning to think it was time at least to undertake a major career reevaluation.

Maybe the time had come for her to grow up.

Jason was starting to seriously worry. C.J. wasn't reacting to Rome and Lyssa the way he'd anticipated. She seemed quiet, almost subdued.

And it hadn't helped that C.J. had retreated to work on that damned computer of hers. What was she typing so industriously? The profile of him? Somehow, he didn't think so. She was up to something, he was sure. The only problem was, what?

The talk of Rome and Lyssa's courtship had brought back painful memories. He remembered what had worried him about Lyssa's resolve to find a family man and marry him. He'd recognized a feminine determination to achieve her goals that was more than daunting to a male—it was downright scary.

His biggest concern, now that he thought about it, was that C.J. showed the same drive to go off around the world that Lyssa had shown in going after her man. And the *really* scary part was that Lyssa had accomplished exactly what she'd set out to do.

Did that mean C.J. was heading off for adventures without him?

And what could he do about it if it did mean exactly that?

Nothing, buddy. That's the bottom line. She has a perfect right to do anything she wants. She doesn't have to stay here with you if she'd rather be roaming the ends of the earth.

His nerves were nearly frazzled by tension. And he was losing his bet with Rome on the outcome of the baseball game, so by the time he wandered into the kitchen to collect a fresh bag of chips, he was primed and ready for a fight. He froze in the doorway.

His three nieces were "helping" their mother

make cookies. And off to the side was C.J., taking pictures with that camera she'd been carrying at the OTL tournament. He hadn't even realized she'd brought it with her.

But then again, he hadn't paid attention to the computer she lugged with her practically everywhere either.

So what's wrong with taking a few snaps of Syd, Sam, and Alex being cute? his logical self argued. *You've taken tons of photos yourself.*

Yeah, but I'm not a reporter. That made all the difference.

When he tuned into the conversation between Lyssa and C.J., his alarm only increased.

"So what do you think, Lyssa? Are you interested?" C.J. leaned forward eagerly, obviously hoping for agreement.

Lyssa swiped a fingerful of dough from the bowl. "I don't know. Let me talk it over with Rome, okay?"

Ice filled Jason's veins. What was C.J. proposing? An article on Lyssa? He certainly hoped not. Knowing his concerns about the profile she was writing about him, C.J. wouldn't even dream of dragging his sister—or his nieces—into a publicity disaster. Would she?

Why all the pictures of the triplets?

"Sure." C.J. shrugged and crouched low to take another snap. "If you think you have to. But it really needs to be your decision."

"How about if I let you know in the next day or so?"

"That's fine. I'll be here till the end of the week."

At that moment the girls spied Jason and ran to him, shrieking with joy. He lifted the first to arrive—Alexandra—and gave her a tight hug. No way was C.J. going to expose his nieces to the nine-day wonder of the public's nosiness. Rome and Lyssa had carefully deflected the curiosity about the trio when the girls were first born, and no way was C.J. going to intrude on them.

No way.

C.J. smiled. "Jason, I was talking to Lyssa about what it was like making the transition from full-time teacher to full-time mother of triplets. I think a lot of people would love to know more about—what's wrong?"

Jason tightened his grip on C.J.'s arm. "Lyssa, C.J. and I have to leave now. We'll talk to you later."

He headed for the door, a protesting C.J. in his wake.

"What's wrong? Why are we going?" She dug in her heels and stopped dead. "Jason, what's going on?"

There were times when intimidation was the only available weapon a beleaguered male had when dealing with a woman too stubborn for her own good. "I told you, we're leaving. Get your stuff and let's go."

"But the game's not over."

"Close enough. Get your stuff."

Lyssa, a worried frown pleating her brow, handed C.J. her purse. "I don't know what's wrong with you, Jason, but you remember your manners."

"Stop mother-henning me. You're my baby sister, remember?" He headed for the door, C.J. still in tow.

"Baby sister or not, if C.J. doesn't want to go with you, she doesn't have to." Lyssa grabbed C.J.'s other arm and held fast. "*Do* you want to go with my caveman brother?"

"I—"

Jason eyed her coldly. "If you want to finish that profile, it's now or never."

He kept his gaze steely, willing her to come with him with no more fuss.

It worked. C.J. smiled at Lyssa. "I'll be fine. Go look after that family of yours."

Lyssa reluctantly released her grip, and Jason hustled C.J. out the door, poking his head back in only long enough to say, "Tell Rome he owes me ten bucks. The Padres are going to whomp the Dodgers, no matter what the score is now. He can pay me next time he sees me."

He drove the short distance home in icy silence, ignoring C.J.'s flustered protests. What he had to say demanded privacy and his full attention. By God, she wasn't going to use his family! Her betrayal, coming so soon after her tacit surrender at the OTL tournament, seemed doubly heinous. He added to her pile of sins her confirmation to Lyssa that she was leaving in only a few more days.

Yes, he had plenty of reason to feel betrayed and put-upon. And he intended to straighten things out with her once and for all.

C.J. tried to decide what she was feeling while Jason hurled the car toward his house. Embarrassment, certainly—Jason had all but dragged her out of the house. Disappointment at his lack of consideration, for sure. But most of all, she realized, she was utterly bewildered. What on earth had happened to make a reasonable, rational man turn into a domineering tyrant in the space of a few minutes?

The only thing she could think of was his concern about the article for *California Business*, but he hadn't mentioned it all day. And, lost in her plans to change her career direction, she certainly hadn't been intruding on his privacy when he started acting so strange. So what had set him off? Surely he didn't know about Wally the Weasel's inclinations toward yellow journalism.

By the time they were inside Jason's house, she had worked herself up to a fine outrage.

"What was that all about?" she demanded as soon as the door closed behind them.

"That's precisely what I wanted to ask you. What the hell do you think you're doing?"

Damn. It *was* about the profile's slant. She straightened her spine and stood toe-to-toe with him. "I am doing my job. Just like everyone else."

"What if I don't want you to do that particular job?"

"*What?* By what right do you even get to express an *opinion* about my job?"

"By the right you gave me—"

"I *never* gave you any rights over me!"

"The hell you didn't. What do you think those kisses we shared meant?"

A wave of heat so strong it blinded her washed up her neck and face. Fury. With extreme effort she corralled her rage and said icily, "They meant that you're California's sexiest businessman. And that's *all*."

"You're saying the other night was nothing but lust? Is that it?"

"Yes!" She prayed her nose hadn't grown so long he could see the lie.

"Hah!" He stomped down the hall. Sam, who came to greet them, meowed a protest, then scurried behind Jason toward the family room. Probably wanted to get a good ringside seat.

Naturally she had to follow. "What do you mean, 'hah'? I'm a perfectly free agent. I decide what I do and where I go. All by myself."

"Just like you make big career decisions without consulting anyone?"

"Wait a second here. That's exactly right. *I* choose how to handle my career. No one else."

Jason had taken up his position at the huge stone fireplace. "When those decisions start affecting me, you'd better start consulting someone. Like me."

"You? What I do has nothing to do with you."

"Sure it does. When you start involving my family, it has a hell of a lot to do with me."

"Your family?" she asked blankly. "What—?"

"Are you, or are you not, proposing to interview Lyssa?" His step forward made her uncomfortably aware of his height and her lack of it.

"Well, yes, but—"

"And were you not taking a boatload of photographs of my nieces?"

"Of course! They're very photogenic."

He folded his arms across his chest. "Right. And a *professional* like you wastes film just to take pictures of some stranger's kids because they're *cute*."

"Yes! It's true."

"Sure." His sarcasm could have shattered a block of ice. "And it has nothing to do with the fact that they're triplets—identical triplets at that."

The reason for his explosion was clear at last to C.J. He thought she intended to exploit his nieces. He thought—well, his thoughts were painfully obvious.

And so was his lack of trust in her.

She reined in her temper and took a deep breath. "Jason, I assure you I mean no harm to Lyssa or her family. I just want to—"

"That's the whole point, isn't it? *You* want. And what anyone else wants doesn't matter. Haven't you learned yet that you can't go through life ignoring other people's needs and desires? Society can't—hell, a *family* can't survive like that."

She stared at him, understanding for perhaps the first time the true depth of the gulf between them. "But I don't have a family. It's just me."

His eyes as bleak as a midwinter's evening, he said, "And you never will have one. You threw away the family you did have, and you're not willing—maybe you're not able—to open yourself up enough to build one of your own."

The pain couldn't have been worse if he'd slashed her with a knife. "I see."

She stepped away from him, ignoring her fingers' burning from the need to reach out to him one last time. Raising her head proudly, she said with icy courtesy, "May I please use your phone to call a cab? I'll find somewhere else to stay tonight."

He hesitated for so long she didn't think he would answer. Finally, he said, "Maybe that would be for the best. I'll give you a lift to the hotel."

But through that cold, silent car ride, check-in at the hotel desk, and a glum ride up the elevator to her room, the only thing that echoed through her mind was the mournful realization that Jason didn't want her near him. He didn't want her around his family.

He simply . . . didn't want her.

EIGHT

By the time the sun peeked in through the curtains of her hotel-room window, C.J.'s mood had shifted from despair to anger. How could Jason show so little trust! He claimed to have faith in other people, yet he'd had none at all in her. Obviously, he was one Prince Charming who owed his pedigree to the amphibian branch of the family.

And she was never big on kissing frogs.

With a big pot of room-service coffee and a cinnamon Danish beside her, she plugged in her laptop and contemplated her plan for the day. She could show up at Jason's office, as scheduled. No doubt she'd be treated to another boring morning of cold-shoulder silence and watching him shuffle papers. No. If she was going to show him how wrong he was, she would need to find another tactic.

It was time to start writing that profile of Mr. I'm-So-Perfectly-Clean-I-Squeak-When-I-Walk Cooper. He expected tabloid trash from her? Well, that's precisely what he was going to get.

And may he choke on it.

Her resolution was interrupted by the shrill ring of her cell phone.

"Hello, Wally." She didn't bother to ask who was calling. Who else could it be?

"Hi, Ceej. Hard at work?" Her editor's voice whined in her ear.

"Sure. You know me. Slaving away and all that."

"Good. How's the article coming?"

"Fine. Just about finished the research for it. Why?"

"You think you can wrap up your profile of Mr. Sexy a bit early? Maybe save us a few bucks on the expense account?"

C.J. pondered. It would be the easy way. She could simply tell Wally that she had all the information she needed to finish the article, then be on the next flight back to the Bay Area. That's all it would take and she'd be out of Jason's life— permanently.

"I'm not quite done here, Wally," she said slowly. "I haven't got enough good pictures."

"Did you try to set up that photo session I mentioned?" Wally's voice was all business.

"Jason Cooper is, um, camera shy. He doesn't like having his picture taken." She could just imagine his reaction to that request from her!

"Sheesh. That's all we need. A cover boy who can't stand to get in front of the camera. You get some good pictures of him before you leave town, you hear me?"

She could almost hear Wally's finger shaking at her. "Sure, Wally. I do have some casual shots," she said, thinking of the pictures she'd taken at the fire—had it only been last Friday? "Will those do?"

"I dunno. Let me think about it."

A rasping sound told her that Wally was scratching his perpetually unshaven chin. She'd heard that the Weasel thought the stubble made him look like Brad Pitt. Fat chance. Wally was in his late fifties and looked every year of it.

"Why don't I see if he'll agree to a photo session?" she offered. "If he says no, well, we can figure it out from there." With any luck, Wally would decide to go with the photos she already had. "In the meantime, I'll get the film I've taken developed and fax a couple of the best shots to you to give you an idea of what they look like."

"Okay. By the way, Ceej . . ."

She *knew* he had something else up his sleeve. "By the way what?"

"Got the word from Mr. Mooney's office this morning first thing. You're being transferred. To the big time. *International Living* is processing the paperwork now for you to sign when you get back."

C.J. stared blankly at the wall where an edge of the wallpaper had started to curl slightly. "You mean they *told* you I asked for a transfer?"

His grating chuckle rasped her nerves. "Ceej, Ceej, Ceej. When you gonna learn that nothing goes on here I don't know about it? Haven't I told you and *told* you that?"

"Sure, Wally." She hesitated. "You're not upset, are you?"

"Naw. It'll be good for you. You show too many scruples. A stint at *IL* will shake some of those out of you." With an abrupt click, he hung up.

You got the job you wanted. You actually got it.

So why didn't she feel happy? Excited? Enthusiastic? Even pleased?

Why did her stomach feel as heavy as her laptop after a hundred-yard sprint through an airport terminal?

A glance at her watch showed her that Jason was probably already at work. Reluctantly, she dragged the phone to her and punched in the phone number for his office.

"Jason Cooper."

How could the mere sound of his voice dry her throat to Gobi aridity?

"Hello?"

"Jason, it's me, C.J.," she blurted before he could hang up.

"Ah." As a response, it was almost totally un-informative.

"I'm, uh, not at your office this morning."

"Really," he drawled. "I hadn't noticed."

Damn him. She firmed her voice to business-like crispness. "I wanted to let you know that I won't have to tag along after you all week as planned. I have almost enough material to do the article now."

"I'm sure you do."

No help there. She took a deep breath. "Yes. Well, one of the things I'm lacking are some photos. Would you be willing to pose for some pictures sometime this week? Perhaps Wednesday after work?"

"You do have the thick skin of a sleazoid reporter, don't you? As it happens, I'm busy Wednesday evening with a prior engagement. And before you ask, any other evening—or day-time—you suggest I will be similarly far too busy to pose for you. Does that clarify the situation?"

"I see." Her hands were shaking like an aspen in fall, but she was proud of her steady voice. "Then I don't believe I'll need to trouble you further." She hung up the phone.

She should have seen it coming. She really should have. There was no realistic way he would agree to do a photo shoot for her. Funny thing was, she believed him when he said he had a prior engagement Wednesday night. Idly she wondered what it was. Taking his nieces to the beach? Conning Rome again on some sports bet?

Dismembering some unfortunate writer?

The whimsy of the last thought had her picking up the phone again, this time to ask for Cora Greene's extension.

"Mr. Cooper's office."

Praying that Jason hadn't bothered to inform his secretary of the estrangement between them, C.J. said in a casual voice, "Hello, Ms. Greene. C. J. Stone here. I'm in a bit of a pickle—my own fault really. I've had to break off my interview with Jason for a couple of days to handle an emergency assignment, but I'll be back late Wednesday. He asked me to meet him at some dinner he's going to attend that night—"

"You mean the Red Cross Blood Donor Awards dinner. Yes, he's representing Golden Auto Parts to collect our Hundred Percent Participation award during the last blood drive."

So he hadn't been lying! "That's the one." C.J. dropped her tone confidentially. "The thing is, I've completely misplaced the directions he gave me for the place and time. I hate to admit it to him—you know how men are when they think women are a bit, well, scatterbrained."

"No problem. I've got the information here." With a precision only a truly magnificent secretary can call on, she listed the details of the dinner. "But, Ms. Stone—"

"Please, call me C.J."

"Certainly, C.J. What I started to say was that you may have a problem getting a ticket to the dinner. Mr. Cooper is scheduled to escort a lady friend, and I believe all the tickets were sold out weeks ago."

Jason had a date with another woman. C.J. forced the information away so she could concentrate on responding. "That's all taken care of. Um, just one favor—"

"Certainly."

"Would you mind not telling Jason that you had to remind me of the dinner? He already thinks I'm a little, uh, . . ." For the life of her, she couldn't think of a good way to end that sentence. Unethical? Irresponsible? Irritating? Insignificant?

The secretary chuckled. "I understand. I won't mention it to him."

Relieved, C.J. said good-bye and hung up.

Now all she had to do was figure out how she could get tickets to a sold-out affair. And while she was at it maybe she could locate some spare courage, because she was sure it would take every speck she could dredge up to watch Jason enjoying the evening with another woman on his arm.

Jason shuffled the Kerlinger contract from the left side of his desk to the right side for the fourth time in twenty minutes. His conversation with C.J. had left him feeling as unsettled as the weather. How did the meteorologists phrase San Diego's standard forecast? Night and morning fog and low clouds, with some clearing along the beaches.

Only problem was the fog and low clouds seemed determined to befuddle his mind all day.

He hadn't slept a wink last night. He wished things were different, wished he'd handled the situation a different way. He wished *she* were different.

Well, wishes and hopes had about as much chance of coming true as a rain dance did of producing a wet day in September.

The truth was, he missed her already. He missed her smile. Her sense of humor. Her bright interest in the world around her. But the even more profound truth was that she wasn't for him. He wanted family, roots, ties. She wanted—demanded—to be unfettered.

I won't need to trouble you further. God, what a cold way to break off a relationship that hadn't had a chance to really get started. Not that his heart recognized that little fact. It didn't matter that they'd barely kissed, never made love, or that his burning curiosity about her had never been satisfied. What did C.J. stand for, anyway? What did she wear to bed?

And how could he live without her?

The ache in his gut was from hunger and weariness, not because his heart was breaking. It had to be. She was out of his life for good, and he could only be glad of that. She wasn't for him. He wasn't for her. They weren't a match. His logic assured him of these truths.

So why did he hurt so bad?

By midafternoon, C.J. had completed the first draft of a profile article on Jason that no doubt would make Wally's whiskers quiver with excitement. It was as slanted, as yellow a piece of journalism as she'd ever read.

She reread the hard copy she'd printed out and shook her head. She could barely stand to read the thing, much less have her byline attached to it. With an extravagant gesture she wadded the printed copy up and pitched it toward the wastebasket.

Naturally, it missed.

She sighed and picked up the crumpled paper, opening it flat and leaving it on the table. She could always toss it later—if she actually found the courage to turn her back on her bread-and-butter job in favor of trying something really daring.

At least her problems with the Wednesday dinner had been solved. Either that, or they'd been doubled, she wasn't exactly sure which. Wally the Weasel had used his friendship with their new publisher to conjure up two tickets for the occasion. So she'd have the unenviable "pleasure" of watching Jason lavish his attention on another woman.

That was the good news.

The bad news was that Stuart Dillman, the magazine's most aggressive, in-your-face photographer, was catching a shuttle flight from the Bay Area Wednesday morning. He was going to attend the dinner with C.J.—thus the two tickets—and would see to it that "appropriate" photographs were taken.

How on earth was she to survive the evening?

Worse, how was Jason going to react when he and his date came face-to-face with the photographer who'd once followed a reluctant female celebrity into the ladies' room to get the "perfect" shot?

After an early and lonely room-service dinner, C.J. realized that she couldn't go through with it. She couldn't write the tripe that Wally wanted, which implied that she couldn't write what *International Living* wanted either. She'd have to go back to the office at the end of the week and turn down that long-sought transfer. She'd probably be fired, but it hardly mattered. She had her savings to fall back on, and that book project. Of course, she wouldn't dare approach Lyssa again, but she'd find other women somewhere who would be happy to participate.

Making that decision lifted a huge weight from her shoulders. It was time she moved on, just as she'd planned. But this time she'd move

up, not out. She'd lift herself and her career to a
new, a higher level. And it wouldn't even mean
she had to leave the country to do so. Oh, not
that she didn't want to see new places. But now
she could look forward to new challenges, right
here in California. Maybe a vacation or two
would fill up those empty passport pages.

Which left only one more thing she needed
to do before she would truly be free to face her
future.

She had to warn Jason about Wednesday
night.

When Jason answered his front door, the last
person he expected to see on his doorstep was
C.J.

"What—what are you doing here?" He actually had to clear his throat because it cracked.

"I wanted to talk to you. May I come in?"

He hesitated. The scent of her still lingered
in the upstairs hallway, despite the fact that he'd
emptied every can of air freshener he could find.
This had to be a mistake.

"Sure." He opened the door wide. *Fool! Have
you no willpower?*

Quietly C.J. led the way to the family room,
where she crouched down to scratch Sam under
his chin. The cat purred loudly. *Traitor!*

"Why are you here?" he asked.

Still crouching, she looked up at him. "First,

I wanted to apologize. I didn't mean to make you angry by taking those photographs of the girls."

He didn't quite know what to say, so he just nodded.

She straightened and reached into the tote bag slung over her shoulder, pulling out a thick package. "Here. This is for you."

"What is it?"

Her tentative smile bubbled straight to his heart. "Open it and see."

Awkwardly, he ripped the newspaper wrapping away and stared at the stationer's box inside. With a questioning glance at her, he opened the box and pulled out . . . "A scrapbook?"

"Look at it," she urged.

Curious now, he opened the book and saw photo after photo of Sydney, Samantha, and Alexandra. The pictures weren't labeled or even permanently mounted, but the collection fully expressed the beauty of the little girls. "These are the pictures you took Sunday."

"Uh-huh," she said. "I had them developed this afternoon. I wanted you to be sure that I wasn't going to put them to nefarious use. The negatives are in the back of the book too."

Automatically he flipped to the final pages. Sure enough, there were the plastic-encased negatives. "I don't understand why you did this."

"I think I wanted you to trust me, if only just a little. I wouldn't hurt your sister's family. I really wouldn't." She took a half step closer and repeated more softly, "Trust me."

He stared at her a long moment, wondering if he dared take that leap of faith. Her eyes pleaded with him for something he didn't know if he could give. But then the memories surfaced—of his frustrated pain all day at work, the lingering scent of her in his house, even the sound of her laugh, and he knew he had no choice.

He put the scrapbook aside and a great sigh heaved his chest. His arms settled around her as naturally as a cat sprawled on a favorite pillow. "I do. God help me, I know it's a mistake, but I do trust you."

Her face nestled against his chest, she asked softly, "Why is it a mistake?"

His hands snuggled her even closer before he tipped her chin up to meet his gaze. "Because you don't yet trust me enough to tell me the truth."

The sudden wariness in her eyes confirmed his assertion. She was holding something back. What, he didn't know. But at this moment he wasn't even sure he cared.

Softly, her face again buried against his neck, she said, "I have another confession to make."

But with her body pressed against his, her breath heating his skin, and her head nestled under his chin, he didn't want to hear any more confessions about how she was going to abandon him at the end of the week. And he certainly could pass up a reminder of how she planned to leave the country within days.

He had the sense that this night—this moment—might be his only chance to be with her. And despite the heartache that was sure to follow, by God he was going to take advantage of the opportunity.

"Shhh," he murmured. "Whatever you're trying to say doesn't matter. Not tonight."

"But—"

His hand pulled her head around so he could stare into her eyes. The syncopated pulse of her heart against his confirmed her—his—excitement. "It doesn't matter—does it?"

Her tongue marked a glistening trail across lips too tempting to ignore. "No," she whispered. "I guess it doesn't. For now."

A great tension left him as he dropped his forehead against hers. "Thank you. I didn't think you'd actually say that. Thank you." He took a deep breath and added, "Just one more thing. Do you want me?"

C.J. smiled. This question was the easiest in the world to answer. Had there been a moment since she met him that she hadn't wanted him?

"Yes," she said, slipping her arms around his neck. "I want you. I want you most of all. More than anything. More than my next breath. More than—"

His mouth stopped the flow of words in a kiss

that was both exquisitely tender and deliciously erotic. Her lips opened under his, inviting entry. When his arms tensed and lifted her, she hung on to his neck, never breaking their kiss.

He carried her down the hall to a room with a huge bed. Dimmed moonlight filtered through curtains, lending the room, the bed, his face, a soft silver glow. He looked magnificent when he slowly lowered her to her feet. He looked like a man she could treasure for this moment—even if she couldn't keep him forever.

Excitement lent urgency to both their movements. Her fingers shook as she unbuttoned his shirt, his trembled as he released her blouse. When he fumbled open the catch to her bra and let it drop to the floor, she felt her chest expand in a long, shaky breath.

His hands cupped her breasts, lifting their pebbled tips toward his mouth. A gasp escaped her as his lips triggered fiery rivers of lava heat from her nipples to her melting feminine core. Lovingly, he explored each swollen peak with his tongue and mouth, suckling and nuzzling until she panted with arousal.

Her hands shaking even harder, she struggled to undo his belt buckle, finally almost ripping it open. With that obstacle removed, she opened his pants just as he released the zipper of her slacks.

Within seconds, their last garments had been discarded and they were lying on that wide, won-

derful bed. Her arms stretched above her head as
he lay on his side beside her. His hands roved the
length of her body, pausing here to tease a response from her, there to caress her into a de-
lighted giggle. She, too, was anxious to explore,
but when her hand encircled him, he gasped and
closed his eyes. Startled, she began to release
him, but his hand held hers in place.

"Don't stop," his husky voice urged. "It just
feels so good."

"I won't," she promised. Encouraged, she caressed every inch of his aroused length, wondering aloud at how miraculously his body altered to
satisfy hers.

He groped in the nightstand and pulled out a
still-wrapped box of condoms. Ripping the
plastic open with his teeth, he managed to get a
foil packet out. He handed it to her. "Help me
put it on," he ordered softly.

Smiling, she took the condom and helped roll
on the protective sheath. He nudged her onto
her back and positioned himself above her. Staring into her eyes, he slowly let himself sink into
her.

"I'd like this moment to last forever. Me en-
tering you. You welcoming me."

It had been a long time for her, and her body
took a moment to adjust to his entry. Still, there
was a sweetness to the event that she, too,
wanted to capture. "I know. It's like being
handed the moon and the stars."

He shifted experimentally, and drew a gasp from her. "Did that hurt?"

She smiled wryly and leaned upward to kiss his mouth. "About as much as my hand hurt you earlier." In truth, nothing had ever felt so good.

He started to move in an increasing rhythm while his words splashed over her skin with hot breaths of excitement. "You're so hot. And wet. And wild. And . . . wonderful."

Their love play went on for what seemed like hours, but must have been mere minutes. Soon, neither could do more than gasp the other's name as pleasure sent them shuddering to a climax almost too great to be borne.

And when he finally withdrew from her and collapsed by her side in a deep, dreamless sleep, C.J. lay awake beside him, her hand capturing the steady beat of his heart under her palm. His loving had imprinted him on her for all time. And when it came time to leave him, as it all too soon would, she would take these few moments of joy with her.

Her remaining days with him could be counted on one hand, yet even if she experienced his loving every one of those nights, it would give her a mere handful of memories to savor in the long months and years ahead.

This tiny taste of ecstasy would have to assuage her aching heart for a long time to come. She wondered if it could possibly be enough.

NINE

C.J. stretched luxuriously, then stopped in mid-yawn as her toe grazed a hairy masculine leg. Her eyes opened wide. There was a man in her bed!

No, wait. She was in *his* bed. An understandable confusion, she admitted silently as she snuggled against Jason. She wasn't used to waking up in someone else's bed. At least, not while that same someone else was in it.

"G'morning." Jason's yawn matched hers for size. He pulled her closer to his side and nuzzled her neck. "Mmmmm. Nice."

His morning stubble rasped against her skin in a sensation that was both erotic and irritating. "Guess it's time to get up," she suggested, wriggling to get away from his scratch-tease nibbles.

"Nope. Not at all." With a smooth move worthy of a contortionist, he pulled her on top of his chest. "Time for some cuddling maybe. But not getting up—at least not in the sense of getting out of bed."

She enjoyed looking down at him. An interesting experience seeing his face sleep-blurred yet full of the sparkle of incipient arousal. And speaking of arousal . . .

She shifted experimentally, eliciting a groan from him. "Don't do that, sweetheart. You might damage something."

"Damage?" she asked sweetly. "You mean you're delicate? And here I thought you were such a big, strong, hunky kind of guy."

His eyebrow quirked upward. "Hunky, huh? I wouldn't want to disappoint you." He fumbled in the nightstand and handed her yet another of those foil packets. When she'd rolled it over him, his hands grasped her hips and guided downward, positioning her just so.

Much later, after a shared shower, they amiably fought over the comics section of the newspaper while munching from bowls of cereal. C.J. had a sudden vision of waking up to the same comfortable routine over and over again. They'd have to get a second newspaper subscription, she pondered, because neither seemed willing to give up the first glimpse at Dilbert and Overboard. And she'd need to invest in some slippers—the tile flooring in the dining room was cold, even on a summer morning.

The sudden realization of the fantasies she

was spinning for herself shocked her motionless. *What on earth are you doing, girl? This isn't forever. The moment he finds out about Stuart Dillman's arrival, your fantasyland will come crashing down around your head in an explosion that will make Hiroshima look like a firecracker.*

"Anything wrong?"

Jason's question pulled her out of her frozen inertia. "No," she said, putting down her spoon. "I, uh, just remembered we never had a chance to finish our talk last night."

He took her hand in his. "Sure we did. Very satisfactorily too." His wicked grin would have sent any sensible duenna scrambling for chastity belts and high, *high* brick walls.

She couldn't possibly keep her mind on the conversation when his finger traced the lines of her palm. She pulled her hand away. "No, we didn't. I wanted to talk to you about the awards dinner you're going to tomorrow night."

"How did you find out about that?"

She shrugged, unwilling to reveal Cora Greene's lapse in confidentiality. "It's not important. It's easy to find out stuff like that. But—"

"I'm sorry, C.J., but I can't take you with me." With a rueful smile, he continued. "I promised an old friend of mine that I'd escort her. She's that former model I told you about whose career was ruined. Well, her real-estate agency is up for an award, just like Golden Auto

Parts, and she asked me if I'd go with her—moral support, you know? You don't mind, do you?"

She shook her head, though visions of impending disaster were starting to form in her mind. She remembered all too well what he'd told her about his friend. Especially the part about how the paparazzi had all but destroyed her life. "It's not that—of course, I don't mind."

"You know I'd rather have you by my side, don't you?"

"Sure. It's okay, really." She gave her best smile—a feeble effort, she feared. Oh, God. How could she possibly confess that he was going to be stalked at that dinner by a photographer aggressive enough to give lessons to the Italian press corps?

Not to mention that she would be standing right by the photographer's side.

Her fantasy visions already turning nightmarish, she frantically searched for a way out of the mess. "Jason, listen, maybe someone else could go to the dinner in your place? How about Rome?"

His brow pleated into a frown. "Why? I promised Naomi I'd take her. She needs my support. I told you she still has a problem with public appearances."

"But couldn't someone else take her? I know it sounds unreasonable to ask, and I really understand that you made the commitment a long time ago, but . . ."

Jason gave her a questioning stare. "What's really going on here? Why don't you want me to go to the dinner?"

Her shrug wouldn't have convinced a six-year-old. "I just think it would be better."

"Better for whom? Me? Or you?"

She stiffened her spine. "Better for both of us."

Jason's gaze dissected her, though she tried to keep hers firm and unwavering. Finally he drawled, "What you really mean is 'better for your article,' isn't it? What about that photo shoot you mentioned yesterday? Have I guessed right?"

Close, but not quite on target. She was trying to keep him out of the camera's lens, not in it. Not that she intended to correct his mistake. "No. You're wrong. I just wish you wouldn't go."

"Well, I'm going anyway. And I don't intend to sit still for any photography session you're cooking up. Don't forget I have to approve your article—and that includes the photographs!"

She couldn't let that pass. "No. You don't have the right to veto anything."

"Are you forgetting the deal we made? You promised to—"

"Let you *see* the article, not let you change it. No one except my editor is allowed to revise my work."

"You're not serious! You know that wasn't what we agreed!"

"I can't help it if you made a mistake in negotiating." Despair gripped her. This whole situation was coming apart at the seams.

Jason obviously echoed her opinion. He stood and stared down at her. "Apparently that's not the only mistake I've made recently. Are you finished eating? I have to get to work."

It was barely seven o'clock and the office was only a ten-minute drive away, but she got the message. He wanted her gone. Again.

"I need to get to work too," she said, clutching her pride around her. "I have an article to write."

"And a reputation to destroy?"

His bitter question burned her like acid. "If that's what you want to think."

"Then get to it. But don't bother showing me what you write. I don't think you'll enjoy having me tear it to shreds in front of you."

As she walked past him tears she refused to let fall burned in her eyes. "You know," she said, pausing by the front door, "you'll look back on this one day soon and realize I tried to do you a favor this morning."

His arrogantly quirked eyebrow was answer enough.

Doggedly she opened the door and walked through it, turning only to explain, "At least I proved to you that I'm no damned good at relationships."

❖━━━━━━━━━━❖

C.J. slowly drove her rental car back to the hotel. Now what? Jason was determined to go to that dinner, and to escort the one woman who would be most affected by Stu's ambush tactics. So how could she possibly prevent a confrontation that could only lead to heartbreak and disappointment all around?

She had one final hope: Keep Stu from coming at all.

Once back in her hotel room, she offered a quick request to her guardian angel and dialed Wally's direct line. He picked it up on the second ring.

"Bates here." Wally's low morning growl reminded her he probably hadn't had enough caffeine yet.

"It's me, C.J."

"Ceej! Whatcha got for me this morning?"

"It's about Stu Dillman's trip down here. Do you really think it's necessary?"

"Oh, yeah. I got those prints you faxed to me yesterday. I'm telling you, kid, you'll have to do much better than this if you're going to be a success at *IL*. There's hardly anything usable in the lot."

She twisted the phone cord around her finger. "What about the one at the fire? Where he's coming out of the building carrying that kid?"

Wally's fingers scraped across his chin.

"Yeah, maybe. But that's about it. And we can't run a feature article with only one picture."

C.J. tried to think of an alternative. "Well, can't you send someone else? Stu's so—"

"He's so damned good, that's what he's 'so'! What's wrong with you this morning?"

What reason could she give? *I'm in love with Jason and it's going to rip my heart out to hurt him?* Sure. Wally would really care. C.J. had yet to see medical proof that the editor possessed any organ resembling a heart.

She crossed her fingers for luck and tried again. "It's just that Stu and I don't exactly get along."

"Hmmm. Not what *he* claims. When he heard about the assignment, he got all excited." Wally's voice sharpened with suspicion. "You two don't have some kind of thing going, do you?"

"No! Of course not!" Her denial blurted out before she realized she'd ruined yet another excuse.

Not that it mattered. "Good. Keep that stuff out of the office, 'cause you still have to work with him."

"But, Wally—"

"Listen, kid, I'll tell you this once. Stu's the best we got. He's also the *only* person available to come down there and save your bacon. So stop whining and get back to work. Write me a bang-

up article so's I can tell the folks over at *IL* how
sorry I am you're leaving."

The phone clicked into silence in her ear. So
much for guardian angels.

She'd run out of options. The dinner tomorrow night was a guaranteed catastrophe. A hol-
low laugh leaked out and echoed in the
impersonal hotel room. At least the event
couldn't be more appropriate.

After all, who better to cope with disaster
than the Red Cross?

Maybe C.J.'s guardian angel hadn't fallen
asleep on the job, she thought when she picked
up Stu Dillman at the airport Wednesday afternoon. She'd run out of possible solutions when
she realized that Jason was away from the office
all day—a courteous way of refusing her phone
calls, she was sure. How could she warn him if he
wouldn't talk to her? It wasn't exactly the kind of
message she could leave with Cora Greene.

Her final hopes seemed destined to dissolve
when she tried to get out of going to the buffet
dinner at all. She had the notion that as long as
Jason didn't see her with Stu, he wouldn't con-
nect it with her, even if he got ambushed. Cow-
ardly hopes, sure, but at this point she was
getting desperate.

She handed the airport parking-gate attendant her parking stub and a dollar. "Stu, about

tonight. You don't need me with you, do you? I'm sure you can get a few pictures on your own."

He rearranged his six-foot-four frame uncomfortably in her budget rental car's passenger seat. "What is this, I-hate-Stu week? I heard you tried to get me off this assignment. Don't you like me anymore?"

She sent him an exasperated glance while maneuvering through the bayside traffic leaving the airport. "Knock it off, Stu. I just don't think you need me tonight."

"Well, babe"—he winced as she narrowly avoided a car that had cut her off—"you're wrong about that. You have to come with me. I need you to point me in the direction of your Mr. Sexy Businessman. I don't know who he is."

She mulled that one over for a moment. "You mean Wally didn't show you a copy of one of the photos I sent him?"

"Nope. Didn't see the Weasel. Just turned in my expenses for my last assignment, grabbed the ticket for San Diego from the lovely Lurlene in the travel department, and ran. Wally had told me you'd fill me in."

This situation had definite possibilities, C.J. realized. Maybe she could conveniently not notice Jason. The charity affair was sold out, so surely there'd be a lot of people roaming around. How hard would it be to miss one particular person in the crowd?

After all, if Stu didn't know whom to ambush, he wouldn't—he couldn't—attack anyone.

Yup, this definitely could work. She sent her guardian angel a congratulatory pat for that inspiration and settled back to explain to Stu where they were going and why.

Her palms slick with perspiration, C.J. handed her ticket to the check-in attendant at the door and walked inside. The enormous ballroom was decorated with red and white balloons and streamers. Small red-and-white-covered tables dotted the middle of the room while various buffet tables lined the edges. At one end, a raised stage held a trendy jazz group playing a variety of what she privately termed "charity-function music." No doubt that was also where the awards would be handed out later in the evening. There was even a tiny square of parquet for dancing just in front of the band.

But best of all, the room's ambience was enhanced by dim lighting and colored spots that roamed over the participants. C.J. suspected she might not recognize her own mother under these circumstances. Perfect.

She wore a long black dress that was old enough to be comfortable and inconspicuous enough to keep her out of the limelight. Stu, unfortunately, had followed his usual flashy dress code. Sure, he wore a tux like the other men, but the sequined lime-green cummerbund and bow tie were dead giveaways that this man had the sartorial sense of a fifteen-year-old.

The only good thing was that C.J. had persuaded him to limit his camera equipment to one thirty-five-millimeter camera with a flash instead of his usual huge bag of equipment.

The crowd of brilliantly plumed attendees swirled in a colorful display. So far, C.J. hadn't caught sight of Jason or his date. And with any luck, she wouldn't.

"Let's head over that way," she suggested to Stu. "I think I see a seafood bar." Like all members of the press, Stu had a fondness for free food. But C.J. knew his special weakness was seafood—and if that particular table was in the farthest, darkest region of the ballroom, well, what a convenient coincidence.

She was beginning to think her guardian angel was doing his magic after all.

But Stu was made of sturdier stuff than she expected. He grabbed a plate of shrimp appetizers in one hand and her arm in the other. "C'mon, C.J., let's circulate a bit. We'll never find him if we hide out in the corner."

Which was exactly her plan. "Um, Stu? It's so dark in here. Maybe we should just wait for him by the crab cakes." She dug in her heels—tough to do in evening pumps—and resisted his pull.

"Listen, babe, I've been on the road for three

weeks straight and I'm pretty shot. I want to get this thing over with early, okay? So let's just find the man, get our snaps, and get back to the hotel so I can crash." His grasp relentlessly pulled her forward.

She was going to bake that guardian angel into the biggest devil's-food cake she could make. *After* she strangled him. Her angel had to be a him because only a male could be this perverse. Her nerves were shot and her stomach tight before the evening had even begun.

C.J. pressed her hand to her forehead, trying to think hard. Jason had told her some story about seafood—no, shellfish. Something about being allergic to it. Was that story about him? Or someone else? Whichever, she had to try.

"Stu, I really think we ought to go back to the seafood table. We'll never find him in this crowd. And he *loves* shrimp and crabs. He's bound to come over to that table sooner or later."

Stu stopped dead. "Gotcha. And it doesn't hurt that we'll get to nosh on the goodies there either, right?"

"Right, Stu." Relieved, she let Stu lead the way back to the dark corner.

Maybe her guardian angel was female after all.

By the time the buffets were picked bare, Stu was getting restless and C.J. was feeling better every moment. Either Jason hadn't come at all or he detested seafood, because she hadn't seen a sign of him or his date.

They had commandeered a small table for two along the wall right beside the buffet table. It was probably the least desirable table in the ballroom as far as seeing the stage was concerned, but it suited C.J.'s needs perfectly. Dark, quiet, and out of the way.

"Stu, maybe he didn't come tonight," she suggested after the cameraman yawned for the fifteenth time. "Why don't we give up and go back to the hotel?"

"Never give up. Hasn't the Weasel explained Persistence 101 to you?" He tipped his glass of iced tea—in contrast to all the stereotypes, he never drank liquor on the job—and took a swallow.

"Yes, but this is dumb. If he's not here, he's not here—"

But her words were interrupted as the speakers boomed into life with an announcement that the awards presentation was about to begin.

Stu perked up. "Didn't you tell me that Mr. Studmuffin was supposed to collect an award tonight?"

Why had she ever mentioned that? "Yes."

"Well, then, all we have to do is wait till his name is called and see if he shows up."

No matter how she tried, C.J. couldn't drill any hole in that plan. Reluctantly, she settled deeper in her chair and hoped that the randomly circling spotlights would keep her in the shadows. Just in case Jason really was nearby.

But fifteen minutes later the dapper announcer called out, "And as special recognition for having every employee participate in our most recent blood drive, two local companies get our Hundred Percent Award. Please come forward, Jason Cooper from Golden Auto Parts, and Naomi Carlysle of Carlysle Realty!"

"Naomi Carlysle?" Stu's ears pricked up visibly. "The former supermodel? What's your studly guy got going with her?" He licked his lips in anticipation. "This has definite promise."

"I don't know," C.J. muttered. She was too busy watching the tall man escort an equally tall, impossibly willowy woman to the front stage. She didn't have to see the man's face to know that Jason had indeed shown up tonight.

Or that he was escorting a woman the fashion magazines had once called the "most beautiful woman in the world."

Stu was already out of his chair, working his way down the side of the room. With the intention of stopping him from doing something crazy—such as the job he was there to do—C.J. followed, muttering "excuse me" and "pardon me" as she tripped over feet along the way.

By the time Stu worked his way to the short steps that led up to the raised stage, C.J. caught up to him. "Stu, wait," she whispered. "This isn't the time—"

"Sure it is, babe."

Jason finished his few words of thanks and stepped back to allow Naomi to speak. But the woman grabbed his hand and kept him beside her.

C.J. was close enough to see the beads of perspiration dotting the woman's brow. She could also see the concern etched into Jason's face as he squeezed his companion's hand reassuringly. The woman was obviously very fragile. Even her amplified voice was barely loud enough to carry to the crowd.

Stu snapped a couple of frames using the bright stage lighting instead of a flash. C.J. was at a loss to know what to do. She felt like someone who was strapped to a runaway locomotive that was about to crash into a wall.

As the announcer handed Jason and Naomi their plaques, they moved toward the stairs where Stu and C.J. lurked. As soon as they moved out of the central spotlight, Naomi sagged heavily against Jason's side. His arm came around her, propping her up, and he bent his head to whisper something into her ear.

"Perfect," Stu whispered. "Now if she'll just cling a bit more . . ."

As if in a bizarre dream, C.J. watched as Naomi stepped closer to the stairs, her free hand coming up to circle Jason's neck and her head drooping against his cheek. From her position a couple feet below the stage, C.J. realized that

Jason's tender hold made him look more like a lover than a concerned friend.

It was perfect tabloid fodder.

C.J. leaned forward to put her hand on Stu's arm. Maybe she could interfere, just enough to salvage the situation. But as Jason and Naomi paused to take the first step down, Stu's flash erupted, brilliantly illuminating the couple's intimate position.

"What the—" Jason's muttered protest died as one of the constantly circling floodlights paused for a crucial second with C.J. in the very center of its beam of light.

She shuddered, her eyes squeezing shut in futile protest. She should have known no good would come of this night. Her presence beside Stu would no doubt seem the ultimate betrayal to Jason. Her every attempt to protect him from this moment had failed.

And as soon as she got her hands on that guardian angel, she was *definitely* going to fricassee him.

TEN

Betrayed again! Damn her! Jason's mental rant-
ings didn't accomplish a thing as he hustled
Naomi off the stage to the anonymous security
of the deserted hall outside the ballroom. C.J.
and that damned photographer had already disappeared. No way would he let her get away with
ambushing him like this, though first he'd have
to see Naomi home.

Then he'd deal with the perfidious C.J.

His temper hadn't cooled in the slightest by
the time he pounded on C.J.'s hotel-room door.
A fifty-dollar bill slipped to the hotel desk clerk
accompanied by a meaningful wink had produced the correct room number. Now it was
time to have things out once and for all.

"Jason! How did you—"

He ignored her and pushed his way inside.
She'd changed out of the slinky black number

she'd worn at the dinner into a pair of jeans and a sweater that matched the amber streaks in her hair. Damn her for being so beautiful his heart ached.

Damn him for noticing.

She closed the door and leaned against it. "Why are you here?"

"Because I want those photographs you took tonight."

"*I* took? I didn't even have a camera."

"Your coconspirator did. I want those negatives."

She shook her head slowly. "I can't do that."

He took a step toward her, bringing all his intimidation to bear. "You mean you won't, not you can't."

She met his stare bravely, but as he'd expected, she looked away first. Brushing past him, she settled into one of the room's two armchairs. If he hadn't noticed the tremor in her hands, he might have thought her unaffected by the situation. He had to work hard to control his own trembling.

Deliberately, he sat in the other chair. With the table between them cluttered with papers and her laptop computer, he might just keep his mind—and his hands—on his goal instead of her.

"What's it going to take to get those pictures? Money? I'll pay anything reasonable."

"Jason, wait. I don't understand why you're

so upset. I know you didn't expect us to be there tonight, but what's the big deal?"

He couldn't sit still. Two steps forward, three back paced him through the entire available floor space of the budget-sized room. How far could he trust her to keep a confidence?

Just as far as you could throw your Explorer. One-armed.

Damn, he hated it when his conscience was smarter than he expected. After four abbreviated trips around the room, he leaned his hands on the arms of her chair. "I can't explain why. But I *need* those pictures back. I have to be sure they're never published."

He barely breathed as he tried to communicate his sincerity to her. Naomi would be devastated if her brand-new and very possessive fiancé saw her apparently canoodling with Jason during the one week he was away. And the man was good for Naomi, Jason could see that. He would do anything to keep from interfering in that relationship.

Apparently his skills at silent communication were about on par with all his others whenever C.J. was around. She shook her head. "I can't get them, Jason. They belong to the magazine."

Frustration erupted within him. With an aggravated swipe, he knocked a pile of papers off the table and stalked to the window.

"Dammit! Not one single thing has gone right since the minute you showed up in my office. I don't understand it. Everything I do falls apart. I try to be boring and a fire breaks out. I try to explain the importance of family and you throw it back in my face. I try to help a friend and end up helping to destroy her—again."

He turned to stare at her. "What have you done to me?"

"What have *I* done? *What have I done?* What about you?" She leaped to her feet and poked him in the chest. "You turn my life upside down without a qualm. You yell at me, try to control my life and my job. You're dangerous."

But Jason wasn't listening. "I don't understand you. You're smart and funny but you don't have a single shred of human emotion inside, do you? You won't listen to reason, you're not willing to bend even an inch to try to rescue what we almost had between us. You're simply willing to chuck everything without even trying to salvage it, just because you don't want ties. Well, listen up, kid, sooner or later *everyone* has ties."

"Not everyone. Not me."

"Then you'll die a lonely embittered old woman."

"Maybe so," she said, "but I won't be turned into anyone's puppet, either."

"You think not?" Jason reached down and grabbed the first set of papers that came to hand, one that had been wadded up and flattened again, and waved it in front of her. "Aren't you a puppet for that scandal sheet you work for? Do you honestly believe that writing crap like this is what you should be wasting your life on?"

She tried to take it back. "Give me that!"

"You're going to publish it so the whole world reads it, right? Why not prove to me that you're proud of what you do? Here." He thrust the papers at her. "Read it aloud to me. Prove to me that you stand behind the lies you write."

She clutched the papers to her chest. "I don't have to. I don't want to."

His laugh was so bitter it burned his throat. "Of course you don't. You're afraid to. All you're interested in is running away because things are a little more difficult than you want. Give me those. *I'll* read it." Before she could protest, he snatched the papers back.

" 'Hunky Golden Auto Parts VP Jason Cooper has more on his mind these days than carburetors and brakes. He keeps a trio of young lovelies busily responding to his every whim. His favorite locales for his revels with these charming beauties are poolside and in the bath, where even a mountain of bubbles can't make this all-male guy one whit less than the essence of masculinity. . . .' "

Disgusted, he tossed the papers on the floor. It was where they belonged—better yet, in an incinerator. He glared at her. "I take it you're referring to my nieces in this?"

Her mouth opened and closed, but she didn't

make a sound. "It's only a first draft," she finally whispered.

"It had better be. If I find one libelous word in the final article, you'll be hearing from my attorney."

Her spine stiffened. "There's not one word in what you read that isn't true."

"*Truth!* What do you know of truth?" He raked his hand through his hair, suddenly tired of it all. "You want to hear some truth? I was beginning to think I loved you. I was beginning to believe you might be brave enough to fight for *us*, instead of for some stupid job that rips apart other people's lives."

"Jason—"

He ruthlessly overrode her protest. "But you don't even see that you've been a coward all along. I know you don't want to write garbage like this. I've known it from the first. But it gives you a way to run from the hard moments so you don't have to face the real world."

"Jason, I—"

He had to finish. "You've been running all your life, haven't you? You ran from your parents because it was too hard to stay and work things out. Now you're running from me, using your stupid job as a shield to protect you against having to make a commitment. That's your pattern, isn't it? Every time someone tries to get close, tries to tie you down in a real relationship, you go running for somewhere else. *How long are you going to keep running away?*"

Without waiting for an answer, he stalked to the door and opened it. He paused, looking back at her. She still stood immobile, though he fancied he could see the sheen of withheld tears. Probably his imagination.

"If you decide to do the decent thing and give me those photos, send them to the office. Otherwise, I don't want to hear from you again."

That shocked her into motion. "Jason, you said . . . you were in love with me?"

He wanted to give her the reassurance she was obviously looking for. He wanted more than anything to make everything better. But there was a gulf between them that she would have to cross, if she were willing to do so. So he said the only thing he could that was both true and final before he left.

"I thought I was."

C.J. didn't sleep at all that night.

He was in love with you, dummy. You let him go.

God, she was an idiot.

But he was always telling you what to do. You'd never be free with him.

Could she live without freedom?

The questions buzzed in her mind till she thought she'd go crazy penned up in the tiny room. Grabbing her purse and room key, she ducked out into the hall. Maybe a walk would clear her head.

She wandered down to the lobby, not sure whether the area around the hotel was safe enough for her to walk around alone at night. But as she approached the desk clerk the all-night gift shop caught her eye and she wandered in there.

She hadn't paid much attention to the amenities of the hotel when she first checked in, and had had little time to do so since. The store shelves were filled with everything a traveler might want, from over-the-counter medications to souvenir T-shirts, from luggage carts to magazines. Idly, she browsed the book rack, but found only techno-thrillers and westerns. She found too-cute-to-buy bottles of sand labeled CALIFORNIA REAL ESTATE and seashells glued and decorated into palm trees.

But none of it served to take her mind off Jason's final devastating words.

I thought I was.

What did he mean by that? That he was mistaken, and he never had loved her? C.J. feared that interpretation even as she acknowledged its probable truth.

Or did he mean that he thought he did, and now he knew?

Had she thrown away the love of a lifetime? And if so, for what?

She dug in her purse and pulled out her unused passport. For this. For the right to keep moving on to new places and new things. New people.

A blur of color caught her eye and she turned to see a pile of stuffed animals. Right on the top of the heap was a gray cat with green eyes that looked so much like Sam that she half expected it to purr. Without hesitation, she grabbed it and took it to the cash register.

She might have to leave Jason behind, but she'd take this cat with her as a reminder of what she almost—might have—had.

Stuffed animal under her arm, she wandered back out of the gift shop, still unwilling to go back to her cell of a room. Her computer lurked there, and that early draft of her profile of Jason. Sooner or later she'd have to face them down, but it would have to be after she built up some courage.

She approached the desk clerk, a young man too skinny for his company blazer. "I was thinking of taking a walk. Is it safe enough for me to go out alone in this area?"

He eyed her sweater and jeans, taking due note of her curves, then glanced at the clock, where the hands neared the witching hour. "I'm afraid I wouldn't recommend it. It's pretty safe around here, but this is an industrial area. There aren't too many streetlights in the area."

She grimaced. "I see. I guess I'll have to work my insomnia off some other way."

"Well . . ." The kid was obviously trying to be helpful. "The pool's closed, of course, and the workout room too. Have you thought of renting a video?" He gestured at the rack of movies gathering dust beside the checkout desk.

"Thanks." She wasn't really in the mood for a movie, but . . . the second cassette from the top was a copy of *It's a Wonderful Life*. The slipcase was both dusty and new-looking, as if this movie had been added to the inventory ages ago and never rented since.

On an impulse, she picked it up and carried it to the clerk. "I'll rent this one, please."

He checked the title, added the charge to her room bill, and handed it back. "I think you're the first person ever to rent this. Everyone hates it."

"Not everyone," she said slowly, thinking of Jason. "For some people, it's their favorite."

Thoughtfully she carried her booty back to her room. A quick detour by the vending area garnered a can of soda and a bag of popcorn she popped in the microwave by the vending machine.

She plunked the gray cat on the bed, collected the papers from the floor and unceremoniously piled them up, and put the tape in the VCR. Settling in the middle of the bed, with one arm around the stuffed animal, and absently munching popcorn and sipping soda, she clicked on the remote to watch the movie from beginning to end.

Maybe this time she could see the message that was so apparent to Jason. Maybe this time she'd understand.

She watched the movie all night long. After the first showing, she rewound the tape and watched it again. Then again. By the time the sun came up, she'd watched the entire movie three times and certain sections several times more.

She finally understood.

In that sweet, simple tale of a man torn between his duty to his family and his desire for freedom, she found herself.

Jason had been right all along, she realized. She *had* spent her life running from the hard things. It was easy to pick up and go somewhere new when times got rough. It was hard to stay and make it work anyway.

George Bailey did it the hard way and won the love of a town.

She'd done it the easy way and won nothing. In fact, she'd thrown away the love of a man who could have been her very own forever love.

With her eyes bloodshot from tears and weariness, she wondered what she ought to do. Her article was due, but not until the end of the week. Besides, she knew now she'd have to write that piece her way, or not at all.

Searching her heart, she knew only one

thing. If she were ever to have a chance to get Jason back, she'd have to take the first step. She'd have to prove to him that she was worthy of that love she'd lost. But how?

After a room-service breakfast and a hot shower, she thought she finally knew the answer.

She packed her bags and checked out of the hotel.

Walking up the familiar sidewalk in Houston, C.J. wondered if she'd ever find the courage to do what had to be done. She'd grown up here among these expensive houses and shady lawns. It was the first place she'd shaken from her feet as a young woman and the last she'd ever expected to come back to.

Her parents' house looked just the same. With a hand that trembled, she pressed the doorbell and heard the remote ding-dong echo inside.

They're not answering. They're not home. You can leave now.

She turned away, then paused. Jason would condemn her for running again. Stubbornly she turned back and pressed the bell again.

She hitched the stuffed cat that hadn't left her side for more than twenty hours tighter under her arm. "What do you think, Sam? Should I stay, or—"

"Hello?" The door had opened and behind

the decorative screen a woman stood. "Who is it?"

C.J. swallowed twice before the sound came out. "Hello, Mother."

"Who on earth . . . ? *C.J.?* What are you doing here?" She nudged the screen door open a crack. "Is something wrong? Do you need money?"

Nice how much confidence they have in you, her cynical self noted. *First thing out of her mouth isn't "how are you" or "come in and give me a hug." It's "do you need money?" Typical.*

C.J. forced the voice to the back of her head. "No, Mother. I'm fine. I just thought I'd stop in to see you and Father. Is that all right?"

"Oh, dear. This *is* awkward."

Her mother looked only slightly older than the last time C.J. had seen her. A few more wrinkles around the eyes perhaps. A slightly thinner hand. Otherwise, the same glossy perfection as always.

"Awkward?" C.J. asked, determined not to give up. *Come back another time,* that same voice urged. *She obviously doesn't want you here. Jason's full of hooey about this family stuff.*

"It isn't that I'm not pleased to see you, dear, but couldn't you have called? It would have prepared me . . . us, for your visit."

C.J. tried not to let the hurt show. So what if she hadn't seen or spoken to her family in half a decade or more? The courtesies must be maintained, after all.

"I'm sorry, Mother. I should have realized I would be imposing. I just had a little free time. It was an impromptu visit to Houston—I didn't have much notice myself. . . ."

The string of useless excuses died. C.J. took a deep breath and tightened her hold on the only family she appeared to have left. A woman could do worse than have a fuzzy gray stuffed cat as companion on her world travels. "I don't mind. I'll come back another day, shall I?"

"No! Don't go!" The screen door flew open, giving C.J. her first good look at her mother. The closer look showed more lines of strain than she'd been able to see through the fuzziness of the screen.

"It's all right," her mother urged. "Come on in. Your father's resting at the moment, but . . ."

She stared at her mother and almost walked in. The temptation to do so was strong, but so was the fear. Did she know enough about family and relationships to make something real this time?

Did she know enough about love?

The last question was the critical one. No. She had no notion of how to build a family—how could she? She'd never seen one in action. Nor did she have the slightest idea how to repair ties that had shriveled and snapped with disuse and mistrust.

So, instead of giving her mother a hug and accepting that invitation, she smiled sadly. "That's all right, Mother. No need to fret. I'll stop by next time I'm in Houston."

"But, C.J.—"

One hand on Sam's fuzzy head, she shook her head. "Give my . . . my love to Father and everyone."

And she walked away.

ELEVEN

C.J. walked away from her parents' house, but she didn't immediately go back to the airport to catch a flight out of town. She could call a cab from a pay phone and head back to the airport. She should do that, in fact.

But she didn't.

Instead she wandered down the street until she came to a familiar hangout from her teenage years—a Waffle House. A slight smile tilting her lips as she walked in and caught a whiff of bacon and maple-flavored syrup, she found a corner booth and settled the stuffed cat beside her while she perused the menu as if she were paying attention to it instead of the bleak thoughts that rattled inside her.

All her life she'd run from anything permanent. She feared she had no skills with which to build a lifelong relationship with anyone, not child-to-parent, not parent-to-child, and certainly not lover-to-lover. She'd shunned anyone who threatened to get too close, to scale the barriers she'd firmly constructed around her heart.

Until Jason.

With effortless ease he'd smashed every one of those barriers. In the space of a few hours she felt as if she'd finally grown up.

When her stomach rumbled for the third time, she decided that hunger didn't clarify her choices any better than the sleepless night before had. She looked at the menu in earnest this time, deliberately choosing a meal that had been her teenage favorite.

She was idly stirring her hot tea when a voice interrupted her thoughts.

"Do you mind if I join you?"

Her mother stood beside the table, looking a bit uncertain of her welcome.

"Sure, Mother," C.J. invited. She gestured at the bench across from her. For some odd reason, it seemed perfectly natural that her mother had shown up here.

"I guess you followed me from the house?" C.J. asked, more to make conversation than anything else.

"Yes. I wanted to see you, even if you didn't have much time before you have to leave."

But once seated, Janine Stone had little to say. The waitress offered a menu and accepted her order of tea, fruit, and English muffin before Janine even met C.J.'s eyes.

"Mother—"

"C.J.—"

C.J. deferred to her mother. "Go ahead."

"C.J., I've wanted to say something to you for a very long time. But it's been so long since you've been home that I . . . Well, I just wanted to say I'm really sorry. I know I—we were a bit hard on you as a child, but . . ."

"Why, Mother? Why were you always like that with me? I don't remember you ever criticizing Louise like that. Why me?"

Janine fiddled with her teacup. "C.J., you were our firstborn. We always knew you were smart. We expected great things of you, wanted great things for you. But you were a difficult child. We never really talked, did we?"

C.J. considered that. No, they never had communicated in any significant way. In fact, she didn't talk about herself with anyone, really. *Except Jason. He was always able to get you to talk. You were a regular blabbermouth around him, weren't you?*

Hastily she shoved that thought away and shook her head.

Her mother explained a bit more. "It's hard being a parent. You want the best for your children, but it's hard to know what that best is. And you were always a quiet little thing. Getting two

consecutive sentences out of you needed a crow-
bar and a pair of pliers."

She acknowledged that with a nod, then
asked, "Mother, why were you and Father so
hard on me when I broke my engagement to
Charles? I expected you to stand by me and—"

"And we didn't." Janine's voice was flat. "I've
always regretted that. But you have to understand how things were with us. Your father's
business was deeply in the red at the time. It
looked like we were going to have to declare
bankruptcy. Then you got engaged to Charles."

A host of clues that she'd barely recognized at
nineteen suddenly coalesced into a complete picture. "And with the prospect of a family tie to us,
Charles's father was willing to help out, wasn't
he?"

"Well, not without a price, darling," her
mother said wryly. "Consolidated Goods owns a
substantial piece of our company these days.
Your father was in the middle of those negotiations when you decided not to marry Charles.
Everything almost fell apart."

"But why didn't you tell me all this at the
time? I would have understood!"

"Would you? At nineteen, when you were at
your most rebellious? When you fought every
single thing we asked of you? And should we
have taken that risk when we were trying so hard
to keep any hint of our financial difficulties from
becoming common knowledge? Even a rumor of

our trouble could have made the difference between disaster and success."

Janine Stone took a sip of tea. "Besides, you refused to explain *why* you wouldn't marry Charles. All you said was no. You never did want to tell us what you truly thought or felt about anything." She smiled sadly. "When you were small, I couldn't even get you to tell me what you wanted for your birthday or Christmas. I always had to guess."

The waitress delivered an omelette for C.J., giving her time to think over her mother's words. Every year she'd resented the inappropriate presents she'd dutifully thanked her parents for. Yet every year she'd refused to offer even a hint that she'd rather have roller skates than a Barbie doll, a bicycle than a party dress.

"You're right, Mother. I guess I never was very good at talking about my feelings. That's why I'm in such trouble now."

She hadn't really meant her mother to hear the last muttered comment, but Janine did. "What trouble?"

C.J. immediately retreated. "Nothing."

Her mother's face crumpled, then the mask of courtesy fitted over it again. "I'm sorry. I'm imposing on you during your meal. I'm not really hungry. I'll—I need to get back home and check on Carl. He'll be wondering where I am." She ran out of her list of excuses, put a twenty-dollar bill on the table, and stood. "At least let me buy your meal. It's the least I can do after—"

"Mother, wait. What's wrong with Father? Why do you have to check on him?"

"I suppose you wouldn't know. He had a heart attack last year, then another last month. We thought we'd lost him."

C.J.'s mouth dropped. She'd never imagined that the world would ever lack her father. He'd always seemed as fixed and immutable as the stars. "Is he all right now?"

"We think so. He's recovering, but it's slow. We have to be careful not to stress him."

"That's why you were so hesitant to let me in at the house, wasn't it? You were afraid the shock of seeing me would—" She couldn't say it. She couldn't even imagine the words that completed that sentence.

"Yes, dear, yes, but not in *that* way. Even a good shock can be dangerous for him. That's why it's so important to prepare him for things."

"Like the prodigal daughter's return." She couldn't help the cynical note to her comment any more than she could keep the lump from her throat.

"If you want to put it that way, yes."

C.J. stared at the woman in front of her, suddenly regretting that she'd rebuffed the first genuine reaching out her mother had allowed herself in years. Maybe in a lifetime. But Janine had already turned away and was getting ready to walk out of her life. Again. Just as she had walked out of Jason's life.

Just as she was always walking away. Alone. Leaving all hope of love and connections behind.

C.J. surged to her feet and put her hand on her mother's arm. "Mother—Mom, don't go. I'm in terrible trouble."

Her mother spun around so fast she almost tripped. "You called me Mom."

That courteous mask had shattered, and for the first time in C.J.'s memory she looked on her mother's face with love. And saw the love shining back toward her. "You're my mom, right? So what else should I call you?"

Her flippancy lent both of them composure, but didn't stop the tears from flowing down her mother's cheeks. Despite that, a watery smile filled her mother's face with a grace C.J. had never noticed before. Her makeup dripping, her eyes reddened with tears, her mother had never looked so lovely.

They sat down again, this time holding each other's hands across the table.

"Tell me about it, C.J. Let me in long enough to try to help you."

Finding the right words was harder than C.J. had expected, but she struggled to explain. "It's a man I know. Jason Cooper. I've made such a terrible mess of things." Urgently, the words tumbling out faster than she could control them, she explained about her turbulent relationship with him.

"He seems like a very nice man from what you've told me."

"Nice?" It seemed an odd description given Jason's fierce anger with C.J.

But Janine's smile turned dreamy. "A woman needs a man to be a knight in shining armor once in a while. One who'll fight to protect her—or fight to keep her. Your Jason seems to have all the proper characteristics."

"Maybe," C.J. said doubtfully. "The thing is, I think I'm in love with him. And . . ." An unexpected sob caught in her throat. "Mom, I've made such a terrible mess of things! I don't know what to do!"

And for the first time in memory, C.J. asked for her mother's advice.

San Diego's famed sunshine glared pitilessly on the man washing the car. Black rings under his eyes betrayed a sleepless night, and a weary slump to his shoulders implied a more profound cheerlessness.

C.J. hesitated, knowing Jason hadn't heard her approach. She'd deliberately parked her rental car far enough from the end of Jason's driveway to ensure he wouldn't notice. That way, if she lost her nerve, she could retreat before he saw her.

Too late. Some sixth sense made him look up at just the wrong time. Steeling her nerve, she walked forward, clutching her large leather folder in sweaty hands.

"Hello, Jason."

He glared back. "What are you doing here?"

"I had to see you."

He picked up a sponge and swiped at the hood of the Explorer. "Why? You made things very clear with that article you wrote. Why the hell should I want to see you again? Why should you want to see me?"

Her knees quivering and about to collapse, she wanted only to run from his harsh bitterness. But the memory of her mother's advice bolstered her courage. "I finished the profile on you."

"Great. Now you can go pillory Lyssa while you're here. Always room for another hatchet job in that scandal sheet you work for, hmm?"

She fumbled in the leather folder and pulled out a few pages of manuscript. Holding them before her like an offering, she took a step closer.

"Don't you want to read it? I promised you I'd let you see it before I sent it in."

A sharp crack of laughter punctuated the splash of the sponge into the bucket of soapy water. "Why bother? As you pointed out last night, it doesn't matter what I think of it, you'll publish it anyway."

This was worse than she'd expected. Maybe she really had ruined things permanently. "What if—what if I agree to let you edit it? You tell me what you want changed and I promise I'll fix it."

He propped his arm on the top of the car's roof and eyed her carefully. "Why would you do that?"

"Because I owe you that much. And more, really."

"Owe me? For what?"

At least his curiosity was overcoming his anger. "Because I just came back from visiting Houston. I—I went to see my parents, and my mother and I had a long talk. My dad is very ill. He's recovering from a couple of heart attacks. And my mother, well, you were right about that, anyway. I did need to make my peace with my parents."

He stared at her as if trying to decipher what that admission could possibly portend, then shook his head and held out his hand.

"Give it to me. I'll read it."

Her hand shook as she placed the article in his. He was careful not to let his fingers touch hers, she noted.

His head bent as he started reading. After the first page, he glanced at her with a stare as penetrating as any laser, but he made no comment. Flipping to the second page, he silently read on.

It was always excruciating for her to watch someone read her work, but to have Jason read this, the most important thing she'd ever written, surely ranked as one of the most refined torments of hell. She shifted from foot to foot, wanting to ask what he thought of it, afraid to find out. She wanted a glass of water. She needed a bathroom. She almost turned and ran.

Yet somehow, she held her ground and waited, mentally reviewing the words she knew by heart.

California's Sexiest Businessman isn't a playboy, or a show-off, or a flirt. He could be any of those things, of course: He's got money, good looks, charm. But Jason Cooper defies the ordinary to be one of California's most extraordinary men.

He's a hero, risking his life to rescue employees from a burning building, then shunning all publicity for his efforts.

He's a family man, spending his free time doting on his toddler nieces instead of dancing till dawn.

He's a loyal friend, protecting those he cares about with his every breath.

Most of all, he's a lover—of old movies, fine cars, a spoiled cat, and one woman who doesn't deserve even a fraction of the love he lavishes on her. . . .

By the time Jason had flipped to the final page, C.J.'s heart was in her throat. When he finished reading the article, he tapped it against the car hood thoughtfully.

"Do you have a pen?"

"What?"

"I have some changes," he said patiently. "Do you have a pen?"

"You want to change it?" Though she parroted the words, they made little sense to her. Why had she never considered this as a possible response? Awkwardly, she scrambled for a pen and handed it to him.

Despair clogging her throat, she watched as he started scribbling on the paper. Beginning with that heartfelt first page, he lined out words here, phrases there, and scratched in others. Too far away and too heartsick to note the specific changes he was making, she concentrated on keeping her composure intact. Obviously, her plan had failed.

With her own stubborn blindness, she really had lost him forever.

She cleared her throat and tried to think of a way to salvage the shreds of pride that remained. "You're proof of that old saying," she said as lightly as she could.

Absently he looked up. "What old saying?"

"That there is no pleasure more profound than changing someone else's writing." She gestured at the marked-up article.

His slashing grin bubbled through her blood. "Yeah. It is kinda fun." He'd reached that last, damning page. He drummed the end of the pen against the paper for a moment, then turned to her. "I need some changes here, too, but I'm not sure . . ."

Her eyes closed in agony. "Wh-what exactly do you want changed?"

She knew what was coming. Sure enough, he read aloud the paragraph she'd most wanted him to accept completely. "You've written, 'But for ladies who would like to meet and keep this extraordinary man, be warned. The author of this article has already staked her claim. Jason Cooper and Carla Janine Stone—' Carla Janine? You were named after your parents? That's why you use your initials?"

She nodded dumbly.

"I always wondered what C.J. stood for. Where was I? Oh, yes. '. . . and Carla Janine Stone will be married by the time this article hits the newsstands. The wedding will be a family affair, held at the bride's family home in Houston.' "

She licked lips as dry as the Sahara. "What do you want changed?"

"Well, what if I don't want us to be married in Houston? What if I want us to be married here in San Diego?"

She lifted her frightened eyes to meet his. Hope and relief flooded through her. Confidently, she stepped forward into the love he showered over her. She put her arms around his neck and promised, "We can be married any-where you want. But my dad is going to give me away, and my mom is going to help me pick out my dress. Okay?"

"And you're not leaving me to wander the world in search of adventure?"

She shook her head as his mouth descended for a kiss. "Never. I don't need to. All the adventure I need is right here in your arms. I'm never going to say good-bye to you again."

"Never?" he asked skeptically.

"Never," she promised. "At least . . ."

"At least what?" he asked, his lips a whisper away from hers.

"At least not if you promise to take me some-where on our honeymoon."

"Like where?" His nibbles along the edge of her mouth made it hard for her to concentrate.

"Oh, I don't know. Paris. London. Rome. Katmandu. Wherever."

Just before his mouth closed firmly over hers, she heard him say, "You've got yourself a deal."

The deal of a lifetime of fun and family—and love.

California's Sexiest Businessman: Jason Cooper

by C. J. Stone-Cooper

California's Sexiest Businessman isn't a playboy, or a show-off, or a flirt. He could be any of those things, of course: He's got money, good looks, charm. But Jason Cooper defies the ordinary to be one of California's most extraordinary men.

He's a hero, risking his life to rescue employees from a burning building, then shunning all publicity for his efforts.

He's a family man, spending his free time doting on his toddler nieces instead of dancing till dawn.

He's a loyal friend, protecting those he cares about with his every breath.

Most of all, he's a lover—of old movies, fine cars, one television-loving gray cat, and one woman who deserves every smidgen of the love he lavishes on her . . .

. . . But for ladies who would like to meet and keep this extraordinary man, be warned. The author of this article has already staked her claim. Jason Cooper and Carla Janine Stone were recently married in a private ceremony in the garden at the bride's family home in Houston.

The groom was attended by Rome Novak, another former Sexiest Businessman, and the bride by her sister, Mrs. Charles Collins. The bride wore her mother's antique silk wedding gown, the third-generation bride to wear the gown at her wedding.

The former Miss Stone was given away by her father, Mr. Carl Stone. The groom's nieces, Samantha, Sydney, and Alexandra Novak, acted as flower girls. And serving as ring bearer was the groom's magnificent gray cat, Samson.

THE EDITORS'
CORNER

For some, March can be one of the coldest months of the season. But those with a heartwarming LOVESWEPT in hand know that it's easy to stay cozy during the harsh winter. This month we're going to take you from peaceful Tylerville, Indiana, to wild Hell, Texas. You'll have a chance to hear the roar of a stadium crowd . . . the irritated grunts of an injured inventor. LOVESWEPT once again covers the spectrum of readers' tastes with this month's batch of romance!

Mary Kay McComas returns with **MS. MILLER AND THE MIDAS MAN,** LOVESWEPT #874. Every time Augusta Miller looks out her kitchen window she sees a huge Rottweiler sitting on her garbage-strewn lawn. Next door, Scotty Hammond smiles each time the same sixteen cans come sailing back over his fence. His plan to meet his new neighbor is a bit unconventional, but Scotty is known all over town for getting things done one way or another. Now he's set his sights on Gus, and she's having no part of it! Can the single dad next door convince the lovely violinist to be his partner in life's duet? Mary Kay is at her best in this hilarious, yet touching story about kindred spirits who have much to learn about love.

Neither Annie Marsden, R.N., nor Link Sheffield, Ph.D., have a high regard for the opposite sex. To Annie, men are competitive macho studs; to Link, women are flighty and irresponsible. Now both are fated to **CHASE THE DREAM,** in LOVESWEPT #875 by Maris Soule. Injured in a lab explosion, a grouchy Link must wait out his recovery before he can get back to his work. Annie has taken care of rude patients before, and the pay for this job as Link's live-in nurse can't be beat. But when new dangers force them into hiding, Annie's job description is drastically altered. Can Annie keep the wary genius safe from the shadows that threaten both their lives? Maris Soule revels in the ultimate mystery of love in this tale of combustible passion and romance on the run.

How far would you be willing to go for a pair of tickets to the hottest game of the season? Domenic Corso and Lynne Stanford are willing to go **THE WHOLE NINE YARDS,** in LOVESWEPT #876 by newcomer Donna Valentino. As die-hard Steelers fans, Dom and Lynne realize their last, best hope of obtaining playoff tickets is to enter the special lottery and apply for a marriage license. The pair had hoped to keep their sweetheart deal a secret, until word of their pending, albeit pretend, nuptials reaches their friends and family! Will this harebrained scheme win them the tickets to the game, or will it succeed in sending them down the aisle for real? Please welcome Donna Valentino as she shows us what happens when a game of let's pretend gives way to something more real than ever imagined!

Hell, Texas. Population 892, that's including the barnyard animals. In Eve Gaddy's **AMAZING GRACE**, LOVESWEPT #877, Max Ridell learns that Hell really does exist. Although after being thrown in jail for defending himself against the town bully, Max is beginning to wish he'd never heard of the one-horse town and its sheriff, Grace O'Malley. Gracie admits that she's not one to stick out in a crowd, but Max makes her want, just once, to be the kind of woman a man could really fall for. Max has a few secrets to hide and Gracie's determined to find out just what's going on in her jurisdiction. Eve Gaddy's tantalizing novel delivers an undercover lawman into the arms of a tenderhearted sheriff and makes for a showdown not to be missed!

Happy reading!

With warmest wishes,

Susann Brailey   *Joy Abella*

Susann Brailey   Joy Abella

Senior Editor   Administrative Editor

P.S. Watch for these Bantam women's fiction titles coming in February! *New York Times* bestselling author Amanda Quick once again stuns the world with

AFFAIR, now available in paperback. Private investigator Charlotte Arkendale doesn't know what to make of Baxter St. Ives, her new man-of-affairs. He claims to be a respectable gentleman, but something in his eyes proclaims otherwise. In **THE RESCUE,** by the versatile Suzanne Robinson, Primrose Adams disappears after witnessing a brutal murder on the streets of Victorian London. But when Sir Luke Hawthorne finds her, Primrose's secret pulls them together in a way neither can imagine. Hailed by *Romantic Times* as an author who "breathes life into an era long since past," Juliana Garnett returns with **THE VOW,** a dazzling medieval tale of intrigue and conquest. When William of Normandy sends his most trusted knight, Luc Louvat, to the northern reaches of Saxon England, Luc finds that it may be a lot more difficult to break down the defenses of a fair maiden than the fortress walls that surround her. And immediately following this page, preview the Bantam women's fiction titles on sale in January!

For current information on Bantam's women's fiction, visit our new Web site, *Isn't It Romantic,* at the following address:

http://www.bdd.com/romance

Don't miss these exciting novels
by your favorite Bantam authors!

On sale in January:

AND THEN YOU DIE . . .

by Iris Johansen

THE EMERALD SWAN

by Jane Feather

A ROSE IN WINTER

by Shana Abé

AND THEN YOU DIE . . .

by *New York Times* bestselling author Iris Johansen

Bess Grady is a hardworking photojournalist on an easy assignment. But what awaits her in a small-town paradise isn't pleasure; it's paralyzing fear. The unimaginable has happened in Tenajo—and Bess and her sister Emily have stumbled right into the middle of it. Suddenly, Emily disappears, Bess is taken captive, and escape seems impossible. But when rescue comes from an unexpected source, Bess is unprepared for the chilling truth. Tenajo was a testing ground—the first stage in a twisted game plan designed to spead terror and destruction. Now, to stop the ruthless conspirators whose next target may be the heartland of the United States, Bess must join forces with the intimidating stranger who led her out of Tenajo, a man whose motives are suspect, whose alliances are unclear, and whose methods have a way of leaving bodies in his wake. For she will do anything—risk everything—to save her sister, her family, and untold thousands of innocent lives.

"You slept well," Emily told Bess. "You look more rested."

"I'll be even more rested by the time we leave here." She met Emily's gaze. "I'm fine. So back off."

Emily smiled. "Eat your breakfast. Rico is already packing up the jeep."

"I'll go help him."

"It's going to be all right, isn't it? We're going to have a good time here."

"If you can keep yourself from—" Oh, what the hell. She wouldn't let this time be spoiled. "You bet. We're going to have a great time."

"And you're glad I came," Emily prompted.

"I'm glad you came."

Emily winked. "Gotcha."

Bess was still smiling as she reached the jeep.

"Ah, you're happy. You slept well?" Rico asked.

She nodded as she stowed her canvas camera case in the jeep. Her gaze went to the hills. "How long has it been since you've been in Tenajo?"

"Almost two years."

"That's a long time. Is your family still there?"

"Just my mother."

"Don't you miss her?"

"I talk to her on the phone every week." He frowned. "My brother and I are doing very well. We could give her a fine apartment in the city, but she would not come. She says it would not be home to her."

She had clearly struck a sore spot. "Evidently someone thinks Tenajo is a wonderful place or Condé Nast wouldn't have sent me."

"Maybe for those who don't have to live there. What does my mother have? Nothing. Not even a washing machine. The people live as they did fifty years ago." He violently slung the last bag into the jeep. "It is the priest's fault. Father Juan has convinced her the city is full of wickedness and greed and she should stay in Tenajo. Stupid old man. There's nothing wrong with having a few comforts."

He was hurting, Bess realized, and she didn't know what to say.

"Maybe I can persuade my mother to come back with me," Rico added.

"I hope so." The words sounded lame even to her. Great, Bess. She searched for some other way to help. "Would you like me to take her photograph? Maybe the two of you together?"

His face lit up. "That would be good. I've only a snapshot my brother took four years ago." He paused. "Maybe you could tell her how well I'm doing in Mexico City. How all the clients ask just for me?" He hurried on, "It would not be a lie. I'm very much in demand."

Her lips twitched. "I'm sure you are." She got into the jeep. "Particularly among the ladies."

He smiled boyishly. "Yes, the ladies are very kind to me. But it would be wiser not to mention that to my mother. She would not understand."

"I'll try to remember," she said solemnly.

"Ready?" Emily had walked to the jeep, and was now handing Rico the box containing the cooking implements. "Let's go. With any luck we'll be in Tenajo by two and I'll be swinging in a hammock by four. I can't wait. I'm sure it's paradise on earth."

Tenajo was not paradise.

It was just a town baking in the afternoon sun. From the hilltop overlooking the town Bess could see a picturesque fountain in the center of the wide cobblestone plaza bordered on three sides by adobe buildings. At the far end of the plaza was a small church.

"Pretty, isn't it?" Emily stood up in the jeep. "Where's the local inn, Rico?"

He pointed at a street off the main thoroughfare. "It's very small but clean."

Emily sighed blissfully. "My hammock is almost in view, Bess."

"I doubt if you could nap with all that caterwauling," Bess said dryly. "You didn't mention the coyotes, Rico. I don't think that—" She stiffened. Oh, God, no. Not coyotes.

Dogs.

She had heard that sound before.

Those were dogs howling. Dozens of dogs. And their mournful, wailing sound was coming from the streets below her.

Bess started to shake.

"What is it?" Emily asked. "What's wrong?"

"Nothing." It couldn't be. It was her imagination. How many times had she awakened in the middle of the night to the howling of those phantom dogs?

"Don't tell me nothing. Are you sick?" Emily demanded.

It wasn't her imagination.

"Danzar." She moistened her lips. "It's crazy but— We have to hurry. *Hurry*, Rico."

Rico stomped on the accelerator, and the jeep careened down the road toward the village.

They didn't see the first body until they were inside the town.

Let Jane Feather capture your heart once again with
the third and final book in her spectacular
"Charm Bracelet Trilogy"

THE EMERALD SWAN

by Jane Feather

Miranda, a gibbering Chip clinging to her neck,
dived into a narrow gap between two houses. It was so
small a space that, even as slight as she was, she had to
stand sideways, pressed between the two walls, barely
able to breathe. Judging by the cesspit stench, the
space was used as a dump for household garbage and
human waste and she found it easier to hold her
breath anyway.

Chip babbled in soft distress, his scrawny little
arms around her neck, his small body shivering with
fear. She stroked his head and neck even while silently
cursing his passion for small shiny objects. He hadn't
intended to steal the woman's comb, but no one had
given her a chance to explain. Chip, fascinated by the
silver glinting in the sunlight, had settled on the
woman's shoulder, sending her into a paroxysm of
panic. He'd tried to reassure her with his interested
chatter as he'd attempted to withdraw the comb from
her elaborate coiffure. He'd only wanted to examine
it more closely, but how to tell that to a hysterical
burgher's wife with prehensile fingers picking
through her hair as if searching for lice?

Miranda had rushed forward to take the monkey

away and immediately the excitable crowd had decided that she and the animal were in cahoots. Miranda, from a working lifetime's familiarity with the various moods of a crowd, had judged discretion to be the better part of valor in this case and had fled, letting loose the entire pack upon her heels.

The baying pack now hurtled in full cry past her hiding place. Chip shivered more violently and babbled his fear softly into her ear. "Shhh." She held him more tightly, waiting until the thudding feet had faded into the distance before sliding out of the narrow space.

"I doubt they'll give up so easily."

She looked up with a start of alarm and saw the gentleman from the quay walking toward her, his scarlet silk cloak billowing behind him. She hadn't paid much attention to his appearance earlier, having merely absorbed the richness of garments that marked him as a nobleman. Now she examined him with rather more care. The silver doublet, black and gold velvet britches, gold stockings and silk cloak indicated a gentleman of considerable substance, as did the rings on his fingers and the silver buckles on his shoes. He wore his black hair curled and cut close to his head and his face was unfashionably clean shaven.

Lazy brown eyes beneath hooded lids regarded her with a glint of amusement and he was smiling slightly, but Miranda couldn't decide whether he was smiling *at* her or *with* her. However, the smile allowed her to see that his mouth was wide and his teeth exceptionally strong and white.

Her own smile was somewhat uncertain. "We didn't steal anything, milord."

"No?" A slender arched black eyebrow lifted.

"No," she stated, flushing. "I am not a thief and

neither is Chip. He's just attracted to things that glitter and he doesn't see why he shouldn't take a closer look."

"Ah." Gareth nodded his understanding. "And I suppose some poor soul objected to the close examination of a monkey?"

Miranda grinned. "Yes, stupid woman. She screamed as if she was being boiled in oil. And the wretched comb was only paste anyway."

"That creature was on her head?" he asked, filled with compassion for the unknown hysteric.

"He's not a creature," Miranda protested. "He's perfectly clean and very good-natured. He wasn't going to hurt her."

"Perhaps the object of his attention didn't know that." The glint of amusement in his lazy regard grew brighter.

"That's always possible," Miranda conceded. "But I was about to take him away and they set on me, so what could I do but run?"

"Quite," he agreed, then cocked his head with a frown at the renewed sounds of a mob in full cry. "But I'm afraid they've realized you gave them the slip."

"Oh, lord of grace," Miranda muttered. "Come on, Chip." She turned to flee but the nobleman reached out and grabbed her arm.

"I have a better idea."

"What?" Miranda looked anxiously over her shoulder toward the sounds of the returning hue and cry.

"You'll be safer if you get off the streets for a while. That orange gown is as distinctive as a beacon. Come with me." He turned back toward the Adam and Eve without waiting for her assent and after an instant's hesitation Miranda followed him, Chip still clinging to her neck.

"Why would you bother with me, milord?" She skipped up beside him, her eyes curious as she looked up at him.

Gareth stared at her. The idea was far from fully formed, but the possibilities beckoned. "Would you be interested in a proposition?"

She looked up at him, and her blue eyes were wary. But she could see nothing in his countenance to alarm her. His brown eyes regarded her calmly, his mouth was relaxed. "A proposition? What kind of a proposition?"

A deeply enthralling, richly romantic novel of
passion and adventure by a stunning new voice in
historical romance . . .

A ROSE IN WINTER

by Shana Abé

*At sixteen, Lady Solange had pledged her love to Damon
Wolf, had dreamed they would be together forever. But
when her ruthless father threatened Damon's life unless
she agreed to marry another, Solange did the only thing
she could: she scorned her true love and sent him
away . . . never imagining the fate that awaited her,
never knowing that one day her destiny would be entwined
with Damon's once more.*

*For nine long years, Solange has lived a nightmare,
wed to a wealthy lord whose handsome face hides a soul of
darkest evil. Yet now, just as she is poised to finally make
good her escape, Damon suddenly appears at the castle gate.
Gone is the gentle hero of her childhood, replaced by a
fiercely attractive, thunderously angry knight, who makes
it clear he has never forgiven her betrayal. Convincing
Damon to escort her to safety will take all Solange's inge-
nuity—but the real challenge lies in breaching the walls
that Damon has built between them, to win back his
trust . . . and his hardened heart.*

Solange.

At last. It was a moment of epiphany. Here she
was in front of him, a grown woman, a widow by her
account. His mind was having a difficult time taking it
all in.

But his body was not, by heaven. He wanted her as fiercely as he ever did. He nearly could not breathe for the want.

He would not crumble, no matter the cost. He wanted to shout at her, he wanted to know why she had rejected him, why she had rejected her father, her homeland. Instead, he kept his lips tightly shut, marking her reaction to his news.

She turned away from him, took a few blind steps to the thronelike chair topping the dais. She did not sit, however, merely stood next to it, arms crossed over her chest. He saw the shiver take her again and again. Her head dipped low.

"My lady," he began.

"My father is dead. The earl is dead. I find—" Her voice broke, a tremulous waver before she recovered. "I find that I cannot think right now. I must rest."

As if on cue, the court women swarmed over to her, taking her arms and leading her down the steps. In frustration, Damon watched them go. He felt robbed of his moment after coming all this way. It couldn't be over this quickly. He would not allow her to disappear just yet.

"Countess," he called.

Solange stopped, then turned. The women fanned around her.

"I am weary," Damon said clearly. "I have traveled far to reach you. I require food and a place to bed for the night."

His words seemed to snap at her, drawing her spine straighter. "Of course. Forgive my poor manners. I'll have one of the men show you to your chambers and arrange to have dinner brought to you. I'm afraid it is past the evening meal, but there is always plenty of food in the buttery."

She murmured instructions to one of the ladies, who curtsied and fluttered away.

"Someone will be with you shortly," she said. "Good eve to you."

They left as a group out the chamber door, a flash of gold in a wash of pastels.

The fire popped and sizzled behind an iron grate, echoing off the emptiness around him.

He was awakened from a sound sleep by a hand placed over his mouth.

In an instant he had drawn the stiletto from beneath the pillow and pressed it against the throat of his attacker. It was a move so deeply ingrained from the years of battle that it took him a full minute to realize that both the hand and the throat belonged to a woman.

To Solange, to be exact.

The dimming fire allowed just enough of the delicacy of her features to stand out in the darkness. She showed no reaction to the sharp dagger but looked down at him calmly, waiting for the recognition to sink in.

He drew the knife back, then pushed her hand away. "Are you mad?"

"Shh. You must speak quietly, lest they hear you."

He tossed the covers off himself and climbed out of the bed. He was almost fully dressed, another habit learned from battle.

"What is the meaning of this, Countess? You have no place here."

"Please, Damon, lower your voice. They must not find us!"

He stared at her in the darkness, baffled. Her urgency was real enough; he reckoned if the newly widowed countess was discovered with another man on the very night of the death of her husband, her reputation would not survive.

The Solange he knew wouldn't have given a shrug of her shoulders over something like her reputation, Yet, she was the countess now.

"Leave," he ordered curtly.

She approached him slowly, hands held out in appeal. "It is my every intention to leave. That is why I'm here."

"What?"

"I want to go with you back to England. I want us to leave here tonight."

He laughed softly. "Your wits are addled, Solange. Go back to your women."

She made an exasperated sound. "The hounds of hell could not drag me back there. I have to go with you, tonight, right now."

She looked so thin and lovely, and very serious. A heavy black cloak swirled around her ankles, but as she moved toward him he saw to his amazement that she was wearing a tunic, hosiery, and buckskin boots: men's clothing. She was still talking.

"We need to leave as soon as you may be ready. I'll help you if you like." In the darkness she took on the earnestness of a young girl, breathless and beguiling. "I can pack very quickly."

He shook his head. "You'll not go anywhere with me, Countess. I'm not courting that kind of trouble. Seek your adventures elsewhere."

She paused, looking as if his barb might have actually hurt. He ignored the flash of guilt. She would not use him, damn her, for whatever game she was playing. He would not submit to that.

"You don't understand." Her voice was subdued. "I have to go."

"And why is that?"

She chewed on her lower lip, another girlish habit he found suddenly annoying. But then her face cleared, became resolute. "If you will not help me, then I will go alone." The cape billowed to life as she swept past him toward an opening in the far wall he had not noticed before.

He caught her before she could vanish into the blackness.

"What is this, madam? You have deliberately put me in a room with hidden doors and secret tunnels? Is it so that you may creep in here in the disguise of nightfall? Is that your amusement these days, Solange?"

"Of course. I knew you would bolt your door closed tonight. How else was I to get in?"

Her look was so innocent, he practically could believe in her virtue again. Amazing, this acting ability she had discovered.

How convenient for her to have a room to keep her lovers nearby, tucked away from prying eyes. What sort of husband had Redmond turned out to be, to allow his wife this unusual freedom in his own home? Damon was almost sorry he could not question him for himself.

"But the man is dead," he muttered. Very interesting.

"Pardon?"

"Your husband. I have just remembered myself. You are a widow driven mad with mourning, no doubt. Someone should be watching over you."

She shook him off with supple strength. "You have changed greatly, Marquess. You should not be surprised to learn that I have changed as well. You speak now of things you could not possibly know anything about. My apologies. I didn't mean to disturb you."

Before he could think to respond, she was gone, her footsteps fading away down the tunnel.

"Damn. Damn, damn, damn."

It was no accident, he knew, that she had chosen to throw back at him his own words from their parting those years past. She was too clever for it to be anything else.

She wasn't really fleeing the estate. She wouldn't act so rashly, he reassured himself. She had nowhere to go that he knew of. It would be a folly beyond belief to think she could make it back to England on her own—a woman, a gentlewoman, who really knew nothing of the ways of the world. She could not be that foolish.

With a muttered oath Damon picked up his scabbard and secured it around his waist. It took only a few minutes to toss his scant belongings back into the traveling sack, but he could feel each second slipping by.

He hurriedly shoved his boots on and laced up the sides. She would be at the stables by now, or who knew where that tunnel let her out of the house. She might have already had a horse waiting in some hidden location, in which case he would have to track her either by sound or wait until dawn, when he could see her horse's prints.

By dawn the entire household would realize their mistress was missing. And who would they first suspect in this dangerous mystery?

On sale in February:

AFFAIR
by Amanda Quick

YOU ONLY LOVE TWICE
by Elizabeth Thornton

THE RESCUE
by Suzanne Robinson

THE VOW
by Juliana Garnett

DON'T MISS THESE FABULOUS
BANTAM WOMEN'S FICTION TITLES